PENNY'S PERCH

TRINA D. ROBINSON

A VOICE IN WRITING, LLC

Published By
A Voice In Writing, LLC
10600 S. Pennsylvania Ave., Ste 16, PMB# 533
Oklahoma City, OK 73170
www.avoiceinwriting.com

Penny's Perch
Copyright © 2021 by Trina D. Robinson

Paperback Edition ISBN: 978-1-7374674-1-0
eBook Edition ISBN: 978-1-7374674-0-3

Library of Congress Control Number: 2021913841

Cover design by izabeladesign
Edited by Misti Long
Author photo by Pernell Images Photography

DEDICATION

I dedicate this book to the roots and branches of my family tree who are not here in the flesh but whose memories I will carry with me forever.

To my mother, Jessie, you were perfection.
To my father, John, I'm still your Trina Bina.
I wish we could have one more conversation.
I love you both, always!

ACKNOWLEDGEMENTS

Thank you Misti Long and everyone in the Write the Book and Write the Vision groups for your encouragement and motivation. Thank you to my friends for supporting me along this journey, those who listened to my elaborate ideas without questioning how or why and those who used their spotlight to brighten mine. To my family, thank you for being my constant, setting the example of living life without boundaries and the unconditional love you've shown this free bird. I am truly blessed!

PENNY'S PERCH

TABLE OF CONTENTS

PAST

There was an intense stare down in the Hamilton kitchen. Covered in apple décor, apple printed drapes and apple colored appliances neatly featured throughout, the place that facilitated many made from scratch meals was a throwback to the black and white TV viewing era. All that was missing was a fresh baked, apple pie cooling on the window ledge. It still needed more time in the oven. Brian, loving son or mama's boy depending on who you asked, stood near the sink. Adjacent to him, by the stove, was his mother, Valerie.

"No, absolutely not, there's no way I'm allowing it, Brian." Valerie stood firm in her decision.

"Ma, you're always talking about tradition. This is a major one. Where's this change coming from?" Brian sought a reason for his mother's shift in attitude.

"She's not the one for you, Son. A mother knows," Valerie responded as she peeked in the oven to check on the pie. "Go set the table, please."

Brian went to the cabinet and retrieved place settings for two as Valerie instructed while he continued their conversation, "Mother, Millicent and I have dated since forever. This was always my plan, graduate from high school, get married, college, start a family. I know how bad you want grandkids. All I need is the family engagement ring."

"Yes, I would love to have grandbabies to spoil," Valerie said as she set the roast down in the center of the table, "but I'm in no rush. Why not wait until after you graduate college so you're certain you're doing the right thing?"

"Ma, I know I'm sure. We've been together—"

"Since forever," Valerie interrupted. "You don't know squat! The only thing you know is that your little teenage hormones need releasing." Valerie looked at her son with a suspicious squint and smirk. Brian gave her an eye-roll and let out an embarrassed sigh at his mother's "little" hormones comment. "Thank God you're waiting until marriage, but you don't know what that ring symbolizes."

"OK Ma, tell me what I don't know. What does the ring symbolize?"

"That ring was passed down to the first wedded Hamilton child since forever." Valerie gave the same faddish pronunciation of the word "forever" as her son. "It's survived segregation, the depression and many wars, both overseas and inside their own four walls. Lasted through many for better or worse and till death do us part." Valerie showed grief in her tone before her straightforwardness returned. "That ring is centuries of love and unbroken promises and just like marriage it should be taken seriously. You don't deal it out like candy on Halloween. Your bride has to deserve it. That girl ain't ready or deserving!" Valerie dropped the homemade biscuits down on the table.

"That girl is the love of my life and she will be my wife, with or without your blessing, ring or no ring." Brian took his seat at the table.

"We'll see about that." Valerie checked on the pie. "Oh shoot!"

"What's wrong?"

"I overcooked the pie." Valerie took the dessert, complete with a deep brown crust and specs of blackened filling, out of the oven and placed it on top of the stove. "This has to be a sign."

Brian rolled his eyes again.

****

Brian tossed and turned in his sleep. He didn't know whether to blame his sleepless night on graduation, proposing, the disagreement with Valerie, proposing with no ring, or his decision to have two slices of the burnt pie. He woke to his mother sitting on the edge of his bed.

"Ma, what are you doing?"

"What I always do, take care of my baby." Valerie pointed to the ring box she placed on Brian's nightstand. "If she's your heart, then she's my heart. If you love her, so do I."

"I do love her, deeply, and she feels the same way. We will be adding to these unbroken promises." Brian picked the ring box up in his hand as he made his declaration and rested it back down. "Thank you, Ma!" Brian gave his mother a forgiving hug.

Though it was nice, the moment felt awkward. Single parent was a title given to Valerie due to circumstances beyond her control. She didn't have to worry about being a working mom. Valerie dedicated her worries to raising Brian right. She mistook toughness for manhood. Neither had seen the vulnerable side of each other before. Once released from the embrace, Valerie walked out of her son's room but not without imparting her motherly advice.

"Just make sure you note in the prenuptial agreement that she has to return the ring when…I mean if you two divorce."

The mood was back to normal.

****

Brian's pulse raced like a feeding hummingbird as he balanced himself on one knee while dressed in his cap and gown. A high school graduate, it was time to focus on striking through another one of his life's goals. He pulled the black, velvet box from his right pants pocket. The weight of its legacy added to the pressure Brian faced to make this moment perfect. As the nineties rhythm and blues soundtrack played in his thoughts and his eyes danced with excitement and apprehension, Brian opened the box. Present, were his mother and future in-laws who stood silent in agreement with smiles draped across their faces. He held the ring in front of the woman he knew he would marry since fourth grade and professed his love.

"Millicent, I remember sitting on the rickety, front steps of my duplex waiting for my buddies to arrive to play video games. I forgot about them when I saw you ride past on your candy apple red bike with basket and streamers. Those colorful strands matched the multi-colored beads in your braided hair with foiled tips. You were the new girl in the neighborhood. I was convinced that day, I was in love and we would always be together. I'm ready for us to start our forever. Millicent Tyler, will you marry me?"

Millicent's delayed response reversed everyone's expression. The diamond's luster didn't represent happily ever after to her. It was an alert to a pre-mature announcement that Millicent was unprepared to answer with yes. She decided to choose logic over love.

"Brian, I'm flattered, but I can't even imagine this level of commitment right now. I got into my first choice university. I'm moving out of state, isn't that amazing!"

Brian retracted the ring and concealed it along with his shattered emotions.

PRESENT

I LOVE YOU

Silence held the Hamilton household captive in the pre-waking hours of Monday morning. Penny used this optimal time to sneak into action. Her tiny feet inched systematically down the stairs. She clinched her toes at the slightest noise, fearful of her capture. The kitchen was Penny's projected location. Her primary target was the refrigerator. She breached the stainless steel appliance and placed her free-flowing curls in front of its bulb as not to let any light escape upstairs. In her signature fashion, adapted from many successful missions, she untwisted the tie on a loaf of bread and grabbed three slices. Before the seals on the fridge touched, Penny reached her hand in an open package of chocolate chip cookies and took two to celebrate her forth-coming good deed. She maneuvered back to her room with the same ninja-like precision she imitated coming downstairs. The five-year-old was prepared to start her day like all others. She would engage her bird friends in deep conversation while she fed them bread and her face with the delectable, sweet treats.

****

Millicent's eyelids popped up like a bagel from a toaster. As she laid face up in bed, she computed the trip to the grocery store, dry cleaners, and Brianna's tutoring session that all needed to be completed by day's end. Light filtered into her bedroom through off-white, sheer curtain panels, bullied by the wind from the open window. She rose with the sun, covered herself with her robe and walked to the breeze and melodic sounds of nature. She forced the curtains to their respective sides, took in a deep breath and exhaled. Her nose turned up at the smell of moisture in the air, but rain was a welcomed forecast to charm away the Southern summer heat.

While reflecting in the window, Millicent's hand slid over a carved heart with the initials B-H + M-H in the frame. This was one of several snubbed memories from her past sprinkled throughout her adopted habitat. Although she hated the constant reminders of her husband's past mistakes, the correct initials were its only reprieve. She closed the window to shut off the world in time to have her beloved start up.

"Millicent, turn off that dang alarm!" Brian sandwiched his head between two pillows and returned to his beauty sleep.

The couple's marriage was well into its itchy stage. During their newlywed phase, Brian and Millicent greeted each other with cute fruit, dessert, and regal nicknames followed by breakfast in bed complete with a rose cut from the bush outside. Millicent felt like a lottery winner after finally being willing and able to marry the only man that held her heart. Their life remained picture perfect until their fifth year of marriage, where the only greetings Millicent received were grumpy moans, loud snoring and farts from her lactose intolerant sweetheart who swallowed milk by the gallon and enjoyed cheese on everything. The rose bush barely bloomed this season and the picture was less than flawless since Brian's employer terminated his position six months ago. Brian was unsuccessful in his attempt to hide his unemployment status from Millicent— a detective without a badge. However, he made her swear never to tell the truth to his mother Valerie—a woman with long reaching apron strings that Brian latched onto for thirty-eight years.

In Valerie's world, she preferred Brian as the corporate success and Millicent the content super wife with a S-W emblazoned on her chest, a mop in one hand and a freshly baked tin of brownies in the other like his first wife, Mari. Although Millicent wore her modern woman crown with pride, she still had southern belle highlights. She took care of home and family while climbing every rung of the corporate ladder. Brian's involuntary plummet in tax bracket placed her as sole breadwinner for them and their daughters, Penny and Brianna. Truthfully, Millicent's finances always sustained the family, especially with the addition of Senior Vice President to her title. At least when Brian worked, he did something other than nothing all day. No amount of coaxing would get him to return to a regular nine to five. He decided to start his own home construction company as his second act. Unfortunately, instead of developing a business plan or scheduling meetings with investors, he slept in.

****

Every droplet of water coming from the shower's head knew its purpose and relaxed all one thousand of Millicent's worked nerves. The aroma of her sweet pea and violet body wash recharged her senses and like the soapy water that camouflaged her curvy frame, all of her worries spiraled down the drain. Stress gurgled its last breath once again.

Millicent placed the bottle of soap back on the shelf with a slim line of residue left at the bottom. She repeated the name as a reminder to add it to the shopping list. With her lips wrapped around her red toothbrush and mouth full of toothpaste, she wiped the steam from the bathroom mirror and confronted the face of a thirty-eight-year-old, natural beauty that discovered her eleventh gray hair three days ago. The frat house atmosphere comprised of Brian and his college friends hanging out every weekend while two underage girls ran wild would leave the average person bald. Hair dye and makeup got all the credit for removing the grays and covering up the frown lines of disbelief from Brian allowing his friends to taunt him into streaking down the block when their team won. No one called the police, the neighbors assumed it was a mental breakdown brought on by his demanding new wife. Millicent suspected it was out of pity. She admired her husband's physique but he mirrored a black Adonis in complexion only. Millicent spat out the toothpaste and replaced her toothbrush in the seashell-studded holder, another snubbed memory from Brian's first honeymoon, then pulled out her miracle bag.

Daytime face applied, Millicent smooched and winked at her reflection as a sign that she was still the fairest of them all. The number of dinner invitations, theater tickets and weekend getaways offered by men she met through work were endless receipts she tucked away in her happiness jar. She turned down every advance with no hesitation because she loved Brian. The same man who hadn't taken her out in months, failed to complement her on new outfits or hairstyles and neglected to mention her being beautiful in two hundred and forty-five days. She was convinced he forgot their anniversary was two weeks away. "Millicent the alarm," exploded out of Brian's mouth from underneath his one thousand thread count safe haven. She hit the snooze button, an honest mistake made as she gave herself another wink.

Millicent turned the alarm off and entered her side of the couple's walk-in closet. She shuffled through her clothes for a cheery blouse. No noticeable sign of stubble meant it was a great day to show off her legs. She swiped through her skirts and found one that matched her chartreuse sleeveless, silk blouse but glitter covered it from Brianna's trial run and sneaky return. Millicent settled for her gray pencil skirt and returned to the bathroom, but she forgot her jewelry. She circled back to pick up her watch—a gift from her parents that she cherished in their memory, her diamond studded earrings and her wedding band. Questions surrounded that piece of metal like vultures to a dying carcass. If she left it behind, would Brian notice? Or, would she have accepted the life sentence if she knew how much maintenance was involved? These queries seemed to be on rotation in Millicent's mind lately. She gagged at the sound of her sleeping Romeo's loud fart and wondered how to turn that off. She shook the nonsense out of her head, slid the ring on her finger and rushed back into the bathroom before the smell escaped the covers.

****

Millicent ventured down the hallway to check-in on the girls prior to cooking breakfast. She found Penny pretending to be asleep on top of her bed covers. Millicent rubbed her tummy, causing the child to giggle.

"I knew you weren't sleep," Millicent divulged. "Get up, dressed, and downstairs for breakfast at seven o'clock."

"School is out for summer vacation," explained Penny, "why do I have to be up so early?"

"Well, the early bird always has its selection of the freshest, yummiest worms."

"But I don't like how worms taste and they are too wiggly."

"Sweetie, it's a cliché." Millicent pushed aside Penny's stuffed animals to sit down on her bed. "It means the earlier you begin your day, the more you are able to get accomplished. Setting goals and accomplishing them is a sign of being a responsible adult."

"I'm not an adult I'm your baby girl, remember? You already told me I wasn't responsible, just like daddy, that's why you won't let me have a dog."

That's not why we don't have a dog, but it is why I should keep certain observations to myself. "Be downstairs by seven, Penny. Do you know when that is?" Millicent pointed to the unicorn-head clock hanging on the wall.

"Yes, when the little sparkly hand is on seven and the big sparkly hand is on twelve."

"Fantastic my lucky Penny, see you at seven o'clock."

Millicent swapped one daughter's bedroom for the other. Brianna's room resembled an outlet mall explosion. Millicent picked up clothes as well as one of her t-shirts that covered the teenager's bedroom floor and added them to an overflowing hamper.

"Why can't you knock," Brianna mumbled in a semi-awake state from underneath her comforter.

"It's my house. I don't have to knock upon entering something I own."

"Your house, that's comical." Brianna rolled on her abdomen and placed a pillow over her head to drown out her stepmother's presence.

I wonder who educated her on that sleep position. "Breakfast will be ready at seven o'clock, don't be late. You know the expression, the early bird's worms are always—"

"You are incredibly corny. Is that what you're cooking? Worms might actually have a more flavorful taste than your usual under-seasoned gruel."

"What lovely compliments a mother gets from her daughter." *She's identical to her father.*

"OMG lady, how many times do I have to explain you're not my mother!"

"Well, I'm the only one around." Millicent punctuated

her comment by slamming Brianna's door closed.

Regretful for her blunt honesty, Millicent tried to remedy the situation and reentered Brianna's bedroom. A pillow thrown like a fastball at her temple thwarted the possibility of peace. Millicent accepted responsibility that she went too far.

"Downstairs at seven, Penny." A command Millicent meant for Brianna.

"What," Penny asked.

"My name is Brianna!" Brianna's door absorbed the hit from a second pillow.

"You know who I meant," Millicent clarified.

"OK," Penny answered.

****

Hunger was next for Millicent to conquer. The power button on the radio mounted underneath the upper kitchen cabinet turned blue and the invited banter between the three co-hosts of her favorite morning radio show pressed through the speakers. The music gave Millicent's feet a rhythm and reason to groove. She high-kicked her way out of her heels and danced back and forth from the refrigerator to the counter as she retrieved all the ingredients for her blues healing Monday morning breakfast. The item she needed to add to the shopping list she forgot, but not her dirty blouses. She shimmied her way to the washer.

Caribbean music played in the background. That, coupled with the footprints left in between the fresh vacuumed lines of the beige living room carpet, took Millicent on a mental trip back to the sandy beaches of Jamaica where she and Brian spent their honeymoon. That passionate escapade seemed like centuries ago. Upside, the carpet looked much better than the dumping ground her husband and kids left her to clean up last night.

"Ouch!" Millicent picked a straggler from her barefoot and regretted buying Penny that pack of unicorns. Her assumption of daughters being more organized than sons was false. It never ceased to amaze Millicent how messy Brianna and Penny were. She convinced herself it was a generational curse from Brian's side of the family. Like a choreographed dance routine, Millicent dumped the contents of her clothes basket into the washer without missing a beat, moved the dial to delicate, pressed start and followed the melody back to the kitchen.

The pilot light flickered from a reddish orange to blue as Millicent prepared a frying pan for the thick cut slices of bacon. Although she was on a diet, the smell of bacon overpowered her expensive perfume on a few occasions. The sizzle of the pork mixed with the bass line of the old school song that played throughout the kitchen. Millicent threw down her apron and her inner dancer took over.

"I'm getting too old for this." Dizzy from the simultaneous spins and kicks, an out of breath Millicent turned her attention back to the stove.

Removing the succulent, dancing swine from the skillet became a religious experience. Millicent prayed the fiery grease didn't pop her in the face or splatter on her outfit. Next, she ladled four round circles of pancake batter onto the preheated griddle. Millicent waited for tiny bubbles to appear on top before she flipped, a tip learned from a trusted TV cook. She searched the granite countertop for the spatula used as a makeshift microphone during her impromptu performance. Millicent figured it was on top of the washer and two-stepped her way back to the laundry room.

The tapping coming from inside the washer had to be the spatula's cry for help. When Millicent lifted the lid on the machine, she found the utensil entangled in a crime scene. In a sea of blood red, Millicent stared in the lifeless eyes of Penny's bodiless baby doll. Undoubtedly, it was a punishment suffered at the hands of Brianna, but it wasn't the real criminal. She fished through her once white blouses and wondered if the culprit was a pair of Brianna's red leggings that had to be washed, Penny's dirty red markers or, she knew the minute she pulled it out, an extra large, fire engine red jersey. This was the third time this month a piece from Brian's wardrobe found its way in with her delicate whites. This burned her up like the unattended pancakes she left on the stove.

Millicent included the scorched pancakes in one of the two putrid smelling garbage bags dumped by the rear door. Last night, she instructed Brian to take them to the curb. No surprise this, like many other things around the house, purposely went undone for her to tackle. Holding the bags at arm's length, Millicent slipped her shoes on and exited the house.

An ovation of chirps welcomed her to the outside world. The host of sparrows that called the family's worn down pergola home attributed to the noise. Their commotion never ended. They squawked all day, seven days a week. One of the territorial creatures even found its way into Brianna's room. When Millicent tried to fan it out, it stood there looking at her as if she didn't belong. She swore it was the same bird lurking around her bedroom window like a thief casing the premises. Perhaps they adjusted to being around humans, but Millicent hadn't adapted to the nostalgia of being around them. She craved the blare of car horns from morning traffic jams, the clamor of partying neighbors through exposed brick walls of her loft apartment, the buzz of attendees and champagne popping at black tie galas. She was a city girl through and through. The suburban lifestyle was a carryover from marriage number one. Mari might have loved the winged pest, but Millicent wished they all would die or fly away.

Millicent tossed the bags in the large, green bin, then dragged it to the curb as the garbage truck rounded the corner. The Hamilton's community consisted of teachers, lawyers, bankers, entrepreneurs and homemakers, all of which reeked of a nauseating bore that intensified from one to the other. Millicent was different. She flaunted her style and intrigue which made her the main talking point of Copper Tree Trail. Whether enjoyable or horrible, Millicent remained indifferent as gossip came with the territory. She was a celebrity even if her house didn't suggest it. The homes in the subdivision were cookie cutter, but the Hamilton's house baked a little too long and called for some needed TLC. Her future homebuilder husband hadn't marked any tasks off his to do list though.

Millicent parked the trash container and returned inside to sanitize her hands and finish breakfast in quiet. The mini fire was enough to paralyze her dancing feet.

****

With the final cup of orange juice filled, the morning rush was complete with only two casualties and a minor flesh wound. This was a record for Millicent who enjoyed a victory sip of juice before the empty seats around her caught her attention. She walked to the bottom of the staircase in an attempt to shepherd her sheep out of their comfortable cocoons.

"Girls, get down here before your breakfast gets cold!"

Brian made his way downstairs led by the smell of food. "Millicent babe, it's the first day of their summer vacation. Let them sleep in."

Millicent worked hard the past year and designed a family schedule that got everyone up, fed and out of the house on time with smiles on their faces. At least, that's what she envisioned on the girl's faces. It was better than the reality of side-eyes and pouted, downturned lips or syrup splattered cheeks. A slacked attitude meant utter chaos come next school term.

"Brian, we have to be persistent with the schedule."

"Millicent, we've become less like a family and more like the Army. What's for breakfast; bacon and eggs, or war rations?"

Criticism was Brian's specialty since his disappearing acts ensured he was nowhere around when things went nuclear. Wife, mother, drill sergeant, coach, referee, and homemaker were the hats that put a crook in Millicent's neck while her husband pretended to be a homebuilder. Brian and Millicent knew each other almost their entire lives, married for seven years, and he seldom constructed a riveting conversation let alone a house. After the nail gun incident, the lawsuit from the broken railing at the community center, the trips to the ER for splinter removals and the concussion; it was beyond Millicent's comprehension that he chose construction as his dream occupation. She pleaded with him numerous times to do something with the pergola that Calverton's sparrow population christened as their nesting motel. He hadn't removed one slat. He insisted it was a great learning opportunity for Penny since it was outside her window. The thought that Penny would learn the facts of life from birds was how Brian's brain operated. He trusted birds, bees, anything or anyone to teach her as long as he wasn't involved in the conversation. He was woozy at the mention of menstrual cycles and birth control when he and Millicent had the talk with Brianna.

Millicent dropped Brian's plate down on the table in front of him. "It's pancakes, bacon and eggs, Dear."

It was time for Millicent to confess and stop pretending. She spent her days trying to make everyone around her happy when she hadn't felt happy for some time. She was tired of repeatedly being on the losing end of compromises. Her marriage dwindled from a blissful love story to a comedy full of ridicule and snappy comebacks. Millicent experienced true joy at work—her escape and the one place she felt appreciated.

Brianna was the first of the sisters to wander into the kitchen with a nodding head that missed the support of her soft pillow. She acknowledged her stepmother and father with a grunt that took fifteen years to materialize.

"Morning, Bri," Millicent greeted as she took her seat at the table. She nearly had a mini-stroke at Brianna's choice of lounging around the house attire. "I know that's not my new, custom designed shirt you're wearing to breakfast. By the way, I appreciate the glitter accents on my skirt you wore and put back without washing."

Brianna's eyes widened. Her foot smashed Millicent's underneath the table because of the secret she spilled. Millicent suppressed the pain. She realized she rightfully chastised Brianna, but it was at the wrong moment.

"What is she doing scavenging around in your closet?" Brian projected a look of disapproval to Millicent then Brianna. "You're not grown, don't start dressing like you are." Brian looked back at Millicent to lash out at her, "It's bad enough you're sashaying out of the house in those skin-tight outfits with no panty lines. I don't want my teenage daughter dressing in the underwear that doesn't make a panty line."

"You mean thongs," Millicent spoke the proper name of the underwear Brian's antiquated lips couldn't pronounce.

"I didn't wear that outdated skirt, Daddy," Brianna corrected Millicent with her father's matching look of displeasure. "It was way too big."

Millicent felt the sting of that low blow, but size never stopped Brianna from wearing her shoes, jewelry, and handbags. Brianna admired Millicent's sense of fashion whether she wanted to admit it or not. This pleased Millicent, which explained why she kept the shared wardrobe and other incidental things Brianna related from Brian. Millicent made a career of battling litigious opponents and could handle the teen. Brian's involvement would only impede Millicent's idea of bonding.

Penny's arrival downstairs was a welcomed conversation stopper. The little girl greeted her father, then her mother with a huge hug.

"You give such good hugs, my lucky Penny. What took you so long to get downstairs?"

"She's been feeding those birds outside her window again," Brianna reported. "If she keeps feeding them, you know they'll never go away."

"I wasn't feeding them!" Aware of the punishment for this action, Penny's tiny palm struck the espresso colored wooden tabletop like a judge's gavel as she objected to her sister's assertion and tried to clear her name. "I was talking to them."

"Cuckoo...Cuckoo," Brianna mocked her sister.

"Cut it out Bri," Millicent demanded. "Sweetie, birds aren't able to talk."

"They chirp, that's talking to them. They're good listeners too, that's why I tell them all my secrets."

What secrets could she possibly be discussing and as a mother, should I be concerned? "Penny, what secrets are you telling them?"

"If I told you, they wouldn't be secrets," Penny pointed out.

"But you're telling the birds," Millicent made her point.

"But who are they going to tell if they can't talk, right Mommy?" Penny's logic left her mother stunned, Brianna impressed and Brian shaking his head.

Millicent dialed back her overprotective mommy mode.

Penny possibly shared stories with her feathered friends about the chocolate cupcake or candy she sneaks into her lunch bag without permission. Although talking to birds was innocent, stealing was probable cause to be alarmed. Likely learned from Brianna, whose recent shoplifting stunt landed her on punishment. The store's owner was sympathetic. He released her over to Millicent and not law enforcement. If the scandal leaked, it would've left a bad mark on Millicent's professional persona and her parental report card. Neighborhood gossip was one thing, mug shots and a juvenile record was a whole other unacceptable scenario.

"Am I the only one who finds this very disturbing," Brianna asked as she waited for the two adults at the table to cosign. "Dad, I think we need to call a psychiatrist."

"I didn't notify a psychiatrist when I caught them flying in and out of your room when you were around Penny's age." Brian gestured his index fingers in the air to enhance his story. "They would be in there so much, I figured you invited them in for a sleepover."

Millicent's smirk offended Brianna more than Penny's outburst of laughter.

"Ha, ha, ha, I never held a conversation with them and I didn't invite them in. Those stupid birds tried to attack me. Not that I want to, I can't talk to birds or anything else with the millions of bees living in those weeds outside my window."

"They're not weeds," Brian corrected Brianna. "They're roses."

"Well, because of those roses and the bees they've attracted, I can't even open my window to get any fresh air in my room. This morning I had to suffer through the smell of burnt pancakes."

"Brian, when are you removing that trellis," Millicent questioned.

"I guess I can have it removed by the end of summer since everyone obviously doesn't like roses except me and your mother," Brian referenced Brianna's biological mother, "God rest her soul."

"Wait!" Brianna changed her mind about the flowers. "Nobody's touching those roses."

"The roses are out of here and it will be before the end of summer." Millicent added another task to Brian's list.

"I wish you were out of here," Brianna mumbled then sulked in her seat with her arms folded.

"Enough with the bratty routine," Brian warned.

Brianna responded, "But Dad, she's always taking away things that mean something to you and me."

"That's it Bri, now eat your breakfast," Brian ended in a stern tone not often used with Princess Brianna.

"Oh yeah, eat the super special breakfast that we've all been summoned here at seven a.m. to partake in when technically only one of us has to be up this early." Brianna cut her eyes to Millicent then looked down at her plate in disgust. "Looks like the same runny eggs to me."

Brian had his limit of sass for the day. "Bri, I've really had all I can take of your attitude. You should be thankful for this and every other meal you receive. Some kids aren't as blessed. Apologize to your mother."

Millicent straightened up in her chair and rested her napkin on her lap. She was elated at Brian's demand for a show of respect toward his wife.

"I'm sorry…Stepmother."

Brianna knew all the right combinations and sucker-punched Millicent with the word she tried to relinquish her from using since she became Mrs. Hamilton. She waited for Brian to come to her rescue again, but he reverted to his powerless human demeanor and instructed the family to bow their heads in prayer.

"Let us pray," Brian started. "God, please make the

pancakes and bacon taste better than the eggs look."

"Amen," Brian, Brianna and Penny responded through their snickers before they dived into their breakfast.

Millicent's eyes scanned the table at her three booby prized possessions and noted their brace filled, coffee stained and toothless grins. She picked up her knife and fork, cut into her delicious eggs and savored the taste that transported her to a more desirable destination. She took a bite of bacon, sipped enough juice to cleanse her palette, patted the corners of her mouth with her napkin before she threw it in Brian's face and excused herself from the table. "I'm leaving for work."

I LOVE YOU NOT

Millicent burned rubber pulling out of her driveway. Like clockwork, her neighbors followed. She fluttered fingers to the left and right as they engaged in their traditional morning ritual. The finger waves were better than the finger gesture Millicent wanted to give them. At least this way she could assure Brian she acknowledged her neighbors every morning even though words never left their mouths unless a newbie or an antsy motorist got out of order.

The neighborhood was its own congested nightmare. There was only one way in and out of the expansive addition. Millicent loved the aesthetics of the big city, but traffic jams before hitting the highway drove her insane. She tried to introduce a system that would alleviate the congestion as part of her household's mandatory contribution to the community at a HOA meeting a couple of years ago. The committee unanimously denied the idea. With another meeting scheduled next Tuesday, Millicent needed to add plates, spoons, forks, and cups to her grocery list.

The Hamilton household went from the house that brought the amazing brownies to the house voted to take care of the paper products and utensils when Millicent came along. There was no guarantee on the purchases or her attendance. Even if Millicent had the time, she wouldn't want to spend it with fanatics of wife number one. Brian wouldn't show up without Millicent. He'd be too afraid he'd have to talk to the neighbors about his business that only existed in his mind. "Let them eat cake out of their hands," Millicent often exclaimed while contemplating what harm the association could do. She concluded the harshest sentence would be to insist they move out of the neighborhood. That would be a dream come true for her.

****

Senior Vice President of Marketing shined on the engraved, metal sign above Millicent's parking space. She delayed catching the elevator to her office and took a detour down the company's Hall of Achievement for a moment of reflection. To see her dreams manifested in the form of plaques, trophies, magazine and newspaper covers that displayed her name or image always shifted her mood.

TRM, Inc. was one of the largest marketing firms in North America. Walking through the doors fifteen years ago as a scared, underpaid intern humbled Millicent. The glass revolving doors welcomed her in, but if she showed any ounce of incompetence, she would leave as fast as she arrived. The company was a recognizable powerhouse and Millicent was well on her way to attaining her ambitious goal of being the one controlling the switch.

Five years after Millicent started her dream job, the company encountered its first blemish. The SEC hit them with embezzlement and money laundering allegations. This forced clients to sever ties and almost annihilated the company's operation. Years after the legal headaches were relieved, Millicent spearheaded a rebranding campaign that regained the trust of those lost and attracted new business. Millicent's natural ability at mending corporate fences wasn't unnoticed by upper management. They granted her free rein over the marketing department.

"Good morning, Mr. Barnes. Can I have a copy of today's paper," Millicent asked.

Tom Barnes owned and operated the newsstand inside

the building. He and his wife celebrated their fiftieth wedding anniversary two weeks ago. Millicent enjoyed seeing the couple have lunch in the cafeteria. He was very attentive and sometimes hand fed his wife. She repaid him with a kiss on his forehead. Their happiness was real and a goal for Millicent.

"Sure, Mrs. Hamilton," Tom handed Millicent the paper. "The cover story is about the fire at the community center, but I'd much rather see your pretty face."

Millicent blushed at Tom's kind words. "How sweet, thank you."

"Your story on the Ice Jazzers partnership's on page seven," Tom mentioned.

"Page seven," Millicent scoffed, "that's an insult! Mr. Barnes we should start a petition, front page headlines only."

"Petition, I've already organized a march." Tom mimicked the motions of a soldier marching in formation.

Millicent and Tom laughed and parted ways as she took the elevator up to her domain.

****

"Good morning, Mrs. Hamilton."

"Good morning, Ryan."

Ryan, better known as Mr. Perfect to all the women in the office, was Millicent's department administrator officially; unofficially, he was the voice of male reasoning and understanding. Outnumbered by a majority female staff, Ryan never hesitated to give his opinion on all things XY chromosome. Twenty years of marriage, father of five, trained chef plus volunteer coach enhanced his wisdom. His highest credential was a wife with the most jubilant smile in the hundreds of photos plastered around his desk.

"You know my homemade danishes you love so much,

I placed one in your office along with a cup of coffee. With school out, I knew you weren't up early making breakfast for you, Brian and the girls."

"Yeah, thanks Ryan," Millicent responded in a rolled eye tone.

Millicent wasn't receptive to others opinions on her family's progression. Everyone wanted her to be easy breezy like Brian who had a tight commitment on being the cool one. A two, relaxed parent household, to Millicent, would be a catastrophe with filth surrounding the entire family as they ate off paper towels in bleach-stained clothes. Although Millicent often vented and criticized Brian's lack of participation, she only trusted her instincts when it came to all things Hamilton. That way, she could take all the credit when things went right.

Millicent entered her office, walked over to her desk and sank down in her plush, Italian leather chair. She turned to the window and looked out at the spectacular view of the city. As she gazed into forever, Millicent forgot about Brian and her kids and reaffirmed to herself that her eggs were the bomb. She closed her eyes, kicked her feet up and soaked in all the peace and quiet.

"What was that?" A loud bang on the windowpane broke Millicent's moment of serenity. She walked to the window where a sparrow flailed about after it flew into the glass.

"Hi, little birdie. What are you doing all the way up here? Are you OK? Did you hurt yourself? You're going to be fine. Wait, am I actually standing here talking to a bird?"

"Penny, what are you doing," Millicent's assistant and childhood friend, Pamela, asked as she walked in.

Millicent switched her name to Penny in the fourth grade as a means of reinventing herself when her parents moved to a new neighborhood in a significantly less populated city. Her old elementary school stretched her patience and Millicent couldn't endure another year of her classmates mocking her real name with lame variations like Millipede, Silly Milli, and the most annoying Mill Dill Pickle. Millicent left her nickname in Thomasville when she traded country for the mature, sophistication of college life in the big city. It wasn't until the birth of her daughter that the memories of her abandoned childhood came racing back. Millicent could not believe her luck. Penny was the nursery rhyme that finally came true, what better way to acknowledge the miracle. Valerie was angry at the choice because she wanted to bestow her granddaughter with a name of higher worth, ancestral background or creativity not the namesake of a woman she couldn't stomach being around for more than a minute. Brian cared less about names and more about the consequences of being out numbered three to one. Mari named their daughter and there was nothing extraordinary or creative about Brian and Marianna becoming Brianna. Creativity did play a part when Pamela was around both Millicent and Penny at the same time in which case Penny, the kid, became Pinwheel. This was to lessen any confusion, at least for Pamela.

"Huh…what," Millicent replied.

"I asked what you're doing."

"I'm looking out the window, Pamela."

"Debating on jumping? Brian called to leave another apology message." Pamela tossed the note on Millicent's desk like a Frisbee. "I figured you had a rough morning again, so spill it."

Brian stayed apologetic about one thing after another rather than stop to think before he opened his mouth and allowed ignorance to fall out. A pitiful dinner usually accompanied his apologies. At least Millicent wouldn't have to worry about what to cook.

"What's that," Pamela asked, as she joined Millicent by

the window.

"A little sparrow had an accident."

"It flew into the window?" Pamela backed up in a frightened manner similar to a cat dreading bath time. "Isn't that a sign of death?"

Millicent played on Pamela's anxiety, "No, it has to be a crow. I've heard that some believe sparrows are spirits of loved ones departed. Did I ever tell you the time my mother found a sparrow in her apartment? She didn't have a chimney, all windows and doors closed; but there it was, in her shower. She believed it was the spirit of my grandfather who recently passed."

"Enough with the ghost stories," Pamela insisted, "let's get back to what's going on with you and Brian."

"It's the same drama different day. Got to love the married life," said Millicent.

"You can love it, I would leave it," Pamela inputted.

Pamela was a two-time divorcee and struggling single mother of three who would still be unemployed if her predecessor decided to stay with the company. Millicent loved her friend; however, Pamela never gave one hundred percent to anything. Her advice went in one ear and out the other. Millicent would fight to the death for her marriage and children. She clearly thought the opponent would be someone other than her husband and kids.

"Thanks for the advice, Pamela, but I think I'll pass."

"Why don't you ask Mrs. Valerie for advice? She is a retired social worker. I'm sure working with Children and Family Services for all those years gave her a great deal of knowledge she'd loved to share, if you'd ask…nicely," Pamela chuckled her way through her comment. The mention of Valerie's name and advice irritated Millicent worse than poison ivy.

Why am I friends with you again, Pamela? "Yeah right, like Valerie would use her powers for good to help me out."

"I thought you and Brian were getting marriage counseling at the church you guys started attending?" Pamela returned to her familiar seat in front of Millicent's desk. "I never really liked Brian anyway. I always thought he was immature."

"Well, some things never change." Millicent sat down in her chair with no chance of regaining that second of introspection. "I don't think counseling is going to work for us either. The pastor keeps bringing up Brian's first marriage."

"What's wrong with that?"

"That's his past. The pastor needs to be concentrating on where we are now."

"Sometimes, before you can move forward you have to take a step back. Look to the past for guidance in your future. It would seem logical that in order to find out what's wrong in your marriage, you would revisit what made his first marriage wonderful."

What would be logical is having your friend's back for once. "Their marriage wasn't that great, Pamela."

"How would you know? You were off earning degrees and living the city life. Those years were the happiest I've ever seen Brian."

"Since when have you been on Mari's side? You know what, never mind. Stop talking about my marriage. Brian and I were destined for one another so I know everything will work its way out. I wish my interactions with Bri were better. It's either the silent treatment or back talk. She's even starting to act up in school. You know Penny's soaking it all in. Bri's the big sister, she should be setting a better example. I don't want Penny picking up her bad habits. I want my little girl to stay sweet and innocent for as long as possible."

"She's been through a lot. Have you considered that?"

Ryan stepped into the room and the conversation. *I forget how well sound travels in this place when I don't close my door.* "Yes, of course I have. Losing a mother is hard, especially at such a tender age, but I'm her mother now. I want us to establish a deeper bond. I want her to feel like she can talk to me about anything, the same way she's gabbing with her girlfriends nonstop. She ignores me, unless it's something she doesn't want her dad to know. She doesn't even call me Mom."

Both self-invited guests, Ryan and Pamela, threw up their hands at Millicent's mom comment.

"You're not her mother," Ryan asserted as he settled into the seat beside Pamela. "Bri will never deny her birth mother and put you in her place, and she shouldn't have to. You need to accept that. Instead of trying to erase her mother, how about you form a relevant relationship with Bri while at the same time keep her real mother's memory alive."

"Why do I have to always bear the burden of my biggest mistake," Millicent asked. "Brian is the one who knew her, keeping her alive should've been his job."

Pamela rolled her eyes. "Sure, give that major responsibility to the immature one."

"Brian has to do some work. I can't keep doing everything," Millicent added.

"But creating an inviting family environment is the most important thing. It's been seven years; honestly, I'm a little shocked and disappointed you haven't figured this out. Forget the designer clothes, cooking their favorite meals, the need for everybody to acknowledge you as Mommy, and make Bri and her mother feel accepted in your new family dynamic. This should be as much your responsibility as Brian's. You can't pick and choose which issues you participate in when you're married. You have to be present 100% of the time, right?" Ryan allowed his question to linger, stood up and left. He handed Millicent her mail, the initial reason for his visit, on his way out.

"Thank you for the mail." Millicent accepted the mail but wished Ryan kept his unsolicited advice.

After Ryan left the room, Millicent returned to her pity party with Pamela.

"Why does she hate me?" Millicent laid her head on her desk.

"She's fifteen, she's a terror. All teenagers are terrors. Trust me, I know. I also know that deep down underneath all the eye rolling, arm folding, foot stomping, stink faces, and out of control hormones there's love. You just have to shake it to the surface sometimes."

Pamela did have a unique talent of finding a punch line in Millicent's problems.

Millicent lifted her head up from her desk. "Yeah, I guess you're right."

"I know I'm right, and you're welcome. See, you don't need a therapist, you need to listen to me more. Let's get back to you and Brian, is he still talking about opening a construction business?"

"Yes, he is."

"You're still against it?"

"Of course, I am. Why couldn't he start his own accounting firm or sports management company, anything other than construction?"

"Construction isn't totally out of his wheelhouse. He and Mari were constantly making improvements to the house. I remember when he built the pergola and they had a barbecue. It was a beautiful day. Mari was an excellent cook. I forgot to get the ingredients to the glaze she used. Did she leave behind a recipe book?"

"I don't know, Pamela."

"Well, can you look?"

"Can you play in traffic or how about shut up about

Mari because I'm sick of it."

"Sorry." There was a short pause before Pamela continued, "He did build all of that furniture for their son. It's a shame you're keeping it hostage in the attic collecting dust."

"It didn't fit my décor."

"Of course, it didn't."

"Pamela, are you going somewhere with this?"

"I'm saying, maybe Brian could have been a great builder in Mari's era. She was more supportive than you."

"She was more supportive than me? All I do is support, but where is my help? Nope Pamela, wrong side again. You can leave." Millicent directed Pamela out of her office with her hands as her eyes scanned her itinerary for the day.

Pamela complied with her boss's request but doubled back for one last thing. "Before I forget, Mr. Jefferson called an emergency meeting today at noon to do a run down on the PiRomEc account. Something about them being entertained by one of our competitors and he wants to make sure we give a flawless performance Wednesday."

"What company has Mr. Jefferson questioning my magic?" Millicent rolled her chair to her wall of mahogany cabinets and pulled out a presentation packet for the meeting. "There's no need to worry because everything is pretty much done. I need you to pick up the samples tomorrow night. Chris promised they will be ready by six-thirty."

"Why do I have to get the samples?"

Millicent converted to serious mode. "Because I'm telling you to get them, that's why!" *Tuesday is family movie night. I have to travel all the way across town to pick up the Chinese food from the only restaurant where Brian and Bri will eat Chinese food. Being your boss has to come with some rewards.* "The shop doesn't open until ten and our meeting is at ten. It's two blocks away from your apartment. Get them Tuesday before you go home, bring them to work Wednesday morning and don't forget. Make that your top priority. Tomorrow, get off work, pick up the samples, then do whatever your heart desires."

"I see why Bri hates you. You're so bossy."

"Pamela," Millicent circled the serious look on her face with her index finger, "I'm not playing. This is a major account for us. Getting it solidifies my place as CEO when Mr. Jefferson retires next year. If we lose it, we'll both be looking for another place to work. Don't forget!"

"I won't forget," Pamela ended.

****

Millicent whipped into her driveway; the only thing on her mind was eating and going to bed. She clicked her garage door opener, nothing happened. When her second try yielded the same conclusion, she remembered batteries needed to go on the shopping list. Millicent honked the horn and hoped someone inside would come out to help. No one showed up. She exited the vehicle, retrieved the dry cleaning from the back seat and laid it over her forearm. She popped the trunk, cradled a large brown paper bag in her free arm and made her way to the front door.

A strange calmness wafted over Millicent as if she entered the wrong home. The TV wasn't blaring and she wasn't being inundated with Penny and Brianna's chorus of she hit me, did not, did to, followed by Brian's bridge of when and what's for dinner.

"Babe, girls, I'm home."

Millicent went into the kitchen shedding her shoes, purse, and laundry along the way. She placed the bag of groceries on the kitchen table and searched around to see what Brian cooked. All she found was a sink full of dirty dishes and a note on the family message board.

> *The girls and I went out for pizza and a movie. Figured you'd need some alone time after what happened this morning. When you get a chance, can you sew the button back on my blue blazer?*

"You've got to be kidding me, alone time? I could see if he booked an evening at the spa, but I'm here hungry, looking at all the things left to clean up, put up and fix. I have enough wiggle room in my diet plan for pizza points, and I've begged him for days to take me to see that new romantic comedy. Unbelievable, I'm the one who's married to him, but the girls get the date night. What am I doing wrong?

Millicent ripped the note from the board, crumpled it into a ball, swished a three-pointer into the kitchen trashcan, reminiscent of her high school point guard days, and put away the groceries. The sudden ring from her home phone caused Millicent to jump. The name on the caller id made her contemplate whether to answer.

"And I thought this day couldn't get any worse." Millicent picked up the receiver and traded her aggravated voice for a calmer one. "Hello, Mother Hamilton. How are you doing this evening?"

Valerie Hamilton and Millicent had a love-hate relationship. Valerie loved to make Millicent's life hell and hated she was nothing like Brian's first wife. She voiced her opinion to Millicent on multiple occasions of how Millicent should be home more for the sake of the girls, how she focused more on her career and how she didn't love her family as much as she loved her job. Valerie even accused her of emasculating Brian by keeping him at home raising the kids, cooking and cleaning while Millicent was off being the man of the house.

"Where's Brian," Valerie snapped back.

"I'm doing well. Brian and the kids went out for dinner and a movie."

"What, too tired to cook for your family?"

Millicent ignored that quip, this time. "Why did you call, Valerie?"

"With the girls being out of school, I came up with a wonderful idea for them to spend their summer vacation in Thomasville with me. It will do them some good to get out of Calverton and get some country air in their lungs. My plane arrives at ten a.m. on Wednesday. I called to make sure someone would be available to pick me up. I'm assuming it will be Brian, or did you quit your job as well to contribute to this ludicrous construction business?"

Millicent questioned Valerie's motive to spend time with the kids. Either this was her way of being family friendly or a deceptive debriefing plot of what was going on in her son's home.

"No, Brian is the one who wants to be the only one profiting from his talent which is why he is establishing his own construction company." Brian would be proud of Millicent's impeccable regurgitation of the explanation he instructed her to memorize. "I still have my job."

"Of course, you do."

"Valerie, I really wished you would've discussed this with Brian and me before you bought the plane tickets. I doubt the girls want to spend two months in Thomasville. You don't have cable and cell phone reception is spotty. I don't see Bri surviving that long. I can't take off to go get them, and Brian may be unavailable. I really wish you would've discussed this with us beforehand."

"First my son, now you're trying to take away my grandchildren."

"Excuse me?"

"Have Brian call me when he gets in. I'll give him my flight details, wouldn't want you to get distracted with work and mess things up. Make sure the girls pack sensible clothes and shoes. If they take any medication, make sure you pack a two-month supply and make a list of any allergies. Also, have the guest room cleaned for my stay. It's a long flight so I'll be ready for a nap as soon as I get in, that is after I have breakfast. I want waffles, sausage, and eggs. No strike that, I've heard about your runny eggs, just waffles, sausage and orange juice—fresh squeezed."

"Wait a minute, there's no way in hello... hello...Valerie?" The harsh dial tone that vibrated Millicent's eardrum signaled the end of her and Valerie's conversation.

"Hey Babe, who are you talking to," Brian asked as he and the girls made it back from their outing.

"It was your mother. She wants you to call her." Millicent noticed Penny slumped over Brian's shoulder. "Bri, take your sister upstairs."

Brian detached Penny's sleeping body from his and handed her to Brianna. Penny wrapped her limbs around her sister as they went upstairs.

"I'll call her in the morning. What's for dinner?"

Millicent wrestled with the childproof top on a bottle of aspirin before responding to Brian. "No, she really wants you to call her tonight. Wait, did you ask me to cook dinner? Didn't you all have pizza?"

"That was like three hours ago, and you haven't eaten. Come on Babe, whip up something real quick. I'm going upstairs to wash up."

"I'm not cooking anything." Millicent ignored her pounding headache and marched up the stairs behind Brian. "I've worked hard all day while you were out playing."

"Playing? I was spending time with our daughters. When was the last time you put that on your itinerary? Maybe, you can try squeezing them in between your extravagant, dinner meetings or golf outings with your male clients."

In a different context, Millicent would feel stoked that her husband felt threatened by her expensed time spent with someone of the opposite sex. Brian accusing her of neglecting the girls because of it was disappointing. This had the scent of Valerie all over it. She found a way of telepathically sending her hate.

"Are you serious? It doesn't matter if I'm sitting at a desk or grabbing a drink at a bar with a client to discuss brand expansion, it's all work that I'm paid very well for by the way. Where do you think the money is coming from to finance those fun times and everything else around here?"

"Don't go there Millicent." Brian retreated into their bedroom.

"Since you're so into time, did you happen to find time today to work on your business plan? If you're serious about starting your own company, you should be putting forth more effort don't you think? Maybe then your meddling mother will get off my back."

"What's your problem with my mother?"

"She hates me! She's coming here Wednesday to get the girls for the summer, and she's going to drive me crazy."

"Babe, I love you; but you're already crazy."

"Grandma's coming to get us? Good! It'll get me away from you feuding four-year-olds." Brianna slammed her bedroom door with such force it slanted the pictures on the hallway walls.

"Slam it again, and I'm taking it off the hinges," Brian yelled in response to Brianna's action.

"Do you need me to look up the instructions," Millicent interjected.

"Not funny." Brian proceeded to the master bathroom.

"Maybe not, but you owning and operating your own construction company is absolutely hilarious." *Did I say that out loud?* Millicent's private thought rolled off her fiery tongue with a trail of sparks targeted at her husband. With a direct hit, Brian stopped on the spot and turned to face his wife with a burned ego.

"Do you think my dream is a joke?"

Millicent went against her battle nature and opted for a kinder approach. "No, I didn't mean that."

"Well, what do you mean? Do you think I'm a joke?"

"No, but what have you built that hasn't fallen apart? The insurance claims alone will bankrupt you in the first quarter. It's not practical."

"Wow Millicent, I'm trying to turn a negative into a positive and I thought you would be happy. For your information, the attic is full of unbroken, furniture made by me if you've ever bothered to look."

"Really, if I bothered to look? When was the last time you went up there and confronted your past, Brian?" Millicent didn't stop for an answer. She had more to get off her chest. "Since when did making baby furniture equal to building houses? Why don't you throw out the construction company idea along with the crap in the attic? That would make me happy."

Brian and Millicent took a pause in their argument after hearing the sound of glass breaking coming from Brianna's room.

"What the heck, Bri?" Brian's only response was the raised volume of the pop song that played on Brianna's stereo. He turned his attention back to his wife. "I guess an unemployed financial analyst who wants to start his own home construction company with no idea of what he's doing might sound a little illogical; but you're supposed to support me no matter what."

"Support, what do you know about support?"

"What are you talking about, Milli?"

"Brian, I do all the cooking, all the cleaning, getting the kids ready for school, helping them with their homework, being the disciplinarian, being your seamstress, along with working ten plus hour days. What do I get in return: no appreciation, back talk, slamming doors, your mother thinks I'm turning you and the girls against her, no support or affection from my husband just flack about my eggs!"

"Your eggs, what in the world do your eggs have to do with anything?"

"My eggs aren't runny, damn it!"

As soon as the words rushed out of Millicent's mouth, she and Brian could do nothing but laugh.

"Millicent, I'm pulling out the white flag. Come here." Brian pulled his wife into his arms and gave her an endearing kiss on the forehead. "It's been hard lately, but I promise you I'll step up with the kids, the company start up, the house duties and my husbandly duties if you know what I mean." Brian ended his conversation and began kissing Millicent all over her face and neck.

Although Millicent enjoyed the sincere moment and flirty attention, it was all too common. Brian tried so hard to meet and even exceed people's expectation of him, often times biting off more than he could chew. Everything would be ideal for a day or more but eventually the pressure boiled over and he had to rob from one to give to the other. It seemed like Millicent's needs and wishes were the ones held up the most. Millicent was famished and didn't have another round in her. She obeyed her husband, and left to go make sandwiches minus the cheese.

****

After putting on her flannel pajama bottoms and one of Brian's old, oversized gamer tees, Millicent removed the decorative pillows from her king-sized bed, pulled back the comforter and flat sheet and crawled in. She gathered her loose curls and pulled them into a high bun, secured it with a clip, and repositioned the covers over half her body. Millicent closed her eyes. Her day stayed active on her mind making it impossible for her to sleep. She stared at the alarm clock on the dresser. Her eyes gradually moved to the family photo and her mind began to wander down a crossroads. *Could I live without them?* Millicent shook the idea out of her head and pulled out her laptop.

Work curbed Millicent's negative thoughts. She sat up in bed, powered up the machine and checked her new emails. She began deleting all the spam when one message from a client, Matt Simon, caught her attention. Millicent read the message to herself, thought it over, and typed a reply.

> *Matt, I have to decline your invitation for drinks and dancing Friday. My husband and I have an engagement. Maybe we can try some other time when we're both available. It's been a pleasure working with you as well. Tell your wife I said hello.*

"And send." Millicent giggled at how fresh Mark came across but needed the ego boost.

"What are you laughing at?" Brian walked into the bedroom with a full belly.

"I replied to my client's email. I mentioned to you the rumors about Matt Simon. Anyway, he sent me the craziest email and—"

"So, my wife is being entertained in our bed by some other man. Isn't that great?" Brian slipped into his side of the closet to change.

"I was laughing at this email he sent me."

Brian continued the conversation from inside the closet, "Well that makes it all better." He emerged in his pajama pants.

Millicent delighted in seeing his four-pack abs and broad, chocolate shoulders. How cunning was Brian to start a fake argument to get her defenses up then cap off the night with a long overdue experience. Instead, he turned off the lights and got into bed with his back turned to her. To Millicent's dismay, the fight was real.

"Brian, what's your problem?"

"The light from your computer, tell your lover goodnight and put it away so I can get some sleep."

Millicent and Brian went from one ridiculous argument into another. Usually, there was a three-day waiting period. Millicent tried to be the bigger person and ignore Brian's childish behavior. She put up her laptop and rested alongside her beloved but she still couldn't sleep. If she couldn't sleep, he wasn't going to sleep either.

"Lover?" Millicent welcomed pettiness in their bed for a ménage à trois. "Are you seriously insinuating that I'm cheating on you?"

"Calm down, I was joking."

"No you're not, because I know when you're joking and when something has your briefs in a bunch. Why you're bothered by it is beyond me, but you're not joking. Like you weren't joking earlier when you implied my outings with clients were getting in the way of me raising the girls. Do you actually think I'm neglecting my family? Brian!"

She nudged Brian's body to get some type of reaction. Brian woke from his micro slumber and turned over to face Millicent. "What!"

"I asked if you think I neglect you and the girls."

"A little," Brian muttered.

"Please explain."

"You never stop working. Like now, even when you're not at work you're working, checking emails and stuff. It's work all the time. I'm not saying you shouldn't have a career." Brian tried to put a cherry on top of his explanation. "I'm saying, maybe this career is becoming much more than you can handle."

"First of all, I've worked my butt off to get where I am in my career because it was what I wanted before anything else. It's not too much for me to handle. It may be too much for you to comprehend. Make no mistake Sweetheart, I can work twenty-two hours a day, come home, cook, clean, tend to the girls, and have you in a fetal position in a deep sleep after screaming my name from the bomb sex I threw down, all before the clock strikes twelve. You'd still be unappreciative. Man, what more do you want from me? Would you rather me be a full time homemaker like Mari with no life of my own just catering to you and the girls? Well, you know what, I already cater to you all and I still have a career, my own identity, my own life."

"For the record, you brought up Mari, not me," Brian clarified.

"Not this time, but I've lost count on how many other times you've made the comparison."

"You can never be Mari, you're Millicent."

"Is that a good thing or bad thing to you?"

"I just want you home more, not obsessed with work and clients," Brian explained.

"OK, so do you want me to quit? We can turn your

construction company dream into a family business."

"That would be welcoming and a big show of support."

Here we go with the support BS again. "What would my role be: Sales, Marketing, Advertising, Vice President, or CEO?"

"I was thinking more administrative."

Millicent shook her head, "You mean woman's work? I can't believe you Brian. When did you become such a He-Man? What has your mother been filling your head with?"

"My mother does not belong in our marital bed."

"You're sounding exactly like her with your archaic views on spousal roles. She is all in between these sheets. Try to get that image out of your thick noggin." Millicent used her index finger like a pin, Brian's head was the cushion that absorbed her multiple pokes.

Brian switched to a more diplomatic tone. "I have a dream of running my business, my way."

"Fine, because I want to run my life, my way."

"Why can't you see my dream, Millicent?"

"Because all you ever do is dream, nothing materializes." *Check* "By the time you wake up, I will have completed three times more than what you merely conceived because..." In true diva fashion, Millicent waited for the suspense of what she would say next build before she finished off Brian. "I'm an accomplisher." *and mate.*

On that note, satisfied with her victory, Millicent turned her back on her husband, pulled the covers over her shoulder and attempted to go to sleep.

Things were far from over for Brian. "Well, congratulations to you. You've fulfilled your dreams. You bring home the bacon, fry it up in a pan and tend to us children. You've definitely earned the right to wear the pants in this household. Now, if you'll excuse me, Sir. I'm certainly not sharing a bed with someone who thinks they have bigger balls than me." Brian jumped out of bed, dropped all the covers to the floor, snatched his pillow and headed for the door.

"Go ahead and go to the guest room. You can stay there when your momma comes since I'm sure you'd prefer to sleep with her anyway!" Millicent's mouth got the best of her again as Brian gave her the customary response—a slammed door.

I WANT A DIVORCE

Millicent stepped out of the elevator on her office floor leaving behind a plume of battlefield dust, courtesy of last night's war with Brian. Tuesday had to be more favorable. That's what Millicent hoped. If the past served as any indication, things could become worse.

"Good morning, Mrs. Hamilton. I have some of my famous apple fritters here, help yourself."

Millicent never noticed how annoyingly cheery Ryan was in the morning. She picked up one of the sweet desserts but put it back down. She searched for a napkin to remove the calorie loaded icing from her fingertips. The last thing Millicent needed was Brian using an expanded waistline as ammunition in their arguments.

"No thanks, Ryan. Brian made breakfast this morning, and I'm stuffed." Millicent rubbed her stomach, mainly to keep her growls from being audible, secondarily to avoid another futile conversation in regards to her personal life. It was time she instituted a new rule of maintaining a professional work relationship at all times. If it wasn't business, it was no one else's business.

"Brian made breakfast?" Pamela followed her nosiness into Millicent's office. "I guess the devil must have his ice skates on because hell has definitely frozen over. Either that or you took my advice and filed for a divorce."

"No one's getting a divorce." Millicent relaxed in her chair and adjusted the lumbar support. Last night's fight was unlike any other. Millicent slept alone for the first time in her marriage. Her spine missed the support of Brian's body.

"Well, we'll see how long this lasts." Pamela tapped her

watch.

"I thought you'd love seeing me come to work with a smile on my face for once. You better get used to it, it may become my new accessory," Millicent replied with optimism even she was skeptical in believing.

"Yeah, yeah, yeah," Pamela returned to her desk.

Millicent turned around in her chair, stared down at the world, and went to her happy place. She wasn't there long. As she watched the bustle of downtown Calverton, the stop and go traffic, and pedestrians rush to their final destinations, she wondered if anyone was happy or were they temporally distracted from their problems.

"The wonderful and considerate Mr. Brian Hamilton is on line one," Pamela's voice echoed over Millicent phone's intercom saturated in cynicism.

"Thank you." Millicent waited a second then picked up the receiver and prepared herself for the sweet talk and sophomore apology Brian had cooked up. She earned a trip to the spa this time. "Hello," Millicent addressed Brian in her I'm still mad at you voice.

"Real mature Millicent, leaving without making breakfast. Plus, Penny's hair was a tangled mess this morning. I had to comb it since you didn't and Bri wouldn't because she accused Penny of getting into the makeup that you bought her again. She even tried to cut one of the girl's pigtails off. We'll talk later about why you think it's appropriate for a fifteen-year-old to have makeup, and it's the expensive kind. Anyway, I got hair gel all over my shirt because our little girl doesn't know the meaning of sit still and hold your head straight. I could cover up the stain but you didn't fix the button on my blazer like I asked you to last night. Keep count Sweetheart, these are all great examples of neglect. Wouldn't you agree?"

He called to yell at her. Millicent's left eye twitched and she could not stop tapping the heel of her shoe on the floor. She didn't know how to respond. Brian infiltrated her job, her domain, her place of peace, to yell at her. The decision for Millicent to engage in those stupid arguments last night was bad, but Brian's counter punch was over the line. She had no time to drown her problems with work because domestic nonsense already had her suffocating.

"Hello...Millicent." Brian waited for his wife to answer.

"Hey Penny," Pamela needed Millicent's assistance.

"Millicent," Brian commanded his wife to respond to him a second time.

"Penny," Pamela entered Millicent's office.

"Mil-li-cent," Brian's irritation grew on his third request for a response.

On the brink of a mental breakdown, Millicent answered her husband first, "Brian, I want a divorce." She then hung up the phone.

"I knew it! Big breakfast my ass. It's about time you started listening to me." Pamela took her usual seat in front of Millicent's desk, ignoring her friend's current mental state. "You know, the guy I met at the gas station has a brother. You want me to hook you up? We can double date like back in the day." Pamela ended with an ear-to-ear grin.

Millicent rolled her eyes at the thought of her double dating like back in her teenage years when Pamela was with some regular Joe and she was with her soul mate whom she just informed she wanted to divorce.

"Get out, Pamela!"

******

Millicent's workday ended too soon. In her eight hours, she managed to save the company thousands in printing cost, closed two deals and negotiated a peace treaty between the feuding ex-lovers in accounting. However, she had no idea what she was going to do when she got home or if she was even going home. She searched through her files for anything that would occupy more of her time.

"Still working," Ryan asked. "Isn't it movie night?"

"Yes Ryan, but I have a lot of work to do...busy, busy, busy. Did you need something?" She figured Pamela spread her news of a divorce throughout the floor so she knew what was coming.

Ryan kept it brief. "No, I'm headed home. I would like to leave you with some advice. No one has a perfect marriage. If you keep striving for perfection, you will be disappointed every time. I hope that helps and eases your jitters of going home."

"Unless you have a whip and chair, I think I'll stay here a little while longer." Millicent remembered her rule and tried to clean up her last statement. "I'm only joking. Everything is fine. Good night, Ryan."

"Good night, Mrs. Hamilton."

Another example of an outsider looking in, Millicent was there in the trenches every day. Total perfection was unattainable; however, 98.99% was a reachable goal if everyone simply listened and did what she assigned them to do. That theory was never going to happen, like divorce was never an option. It wasn't a ploy to make one act right either. Lonely, single woman nights in the big city flashed in Millicent's head along with the notions of being a single mother while operating a Fortune 500 company and what would happen if she left Brianna in the care of Brian and Valerie.

Millicent's stiletto-tipped, manicured nails were anxious for contact as they tapped on her forearm, knee and keyboard. In need to find something other than irrational thoughts to occupy her mind, she checked her emails one last time. When she ended that task, she rearranged the items on her desk. As the sun set, the last of its rays glared off her family portrait she had framed to match the contemporary décor in her office. This gave Millicent clear instructions.

I need to go home to my husband and kids.

****

Millicent pulled into the driveway of the home she knew. Gunshot rounds and air strike commands blared from within accompanied by the sound of sinister laughter and screams for mercy. She snuck into the kitchen through the side door and placed the Chinese takeout on the counter. She went to retrieve plates from the cabinet but stopped short at the sound of a blood-curdling scream from Penny.

"Daddy, Bri pinched me and I'm bleeding!"

"I told her to stay out of my stuff!" Brianna justified her actions from her bedroom before she slammed the door.

Penny ran to her father to show him her injuries. "Daddy look, I'm bleeding! I need to go to the emergency room."

Brian pressed pause on his game. He looked at the small droplets of blood on Penny's forearm and dismissed his daughter's plea for an ER visit. "It's a scratch, Penny. Go put a bandage on it." Brian returned to his military mission.

Penny fell down on the floor kicking and screaming, "Daddy, I'm dying! You're going to let me bleed to death! I want Mommy!"

Penny's screams were sure to alarm the neighbors, so Brian stopped his game for an unprecedented second time to get the First Aid Kit out of the kitchen. He maneuvered his way around Penny who was still on the floor resembling a bug on its back struggling to right itself.

Millicent met him in passing, handed him a Band-Aid and motioned that dinner was on the table as she escaped upstairs with a box of fried rice, two bowls of sesame chicken and two pairs of chopsticks in hand. Penny let her mother get by her unnoticed but the smell of Chinese food healed her from her life threatening injury.

Penny jumped to her feet, "Chinese food! Yes! Yes! Yes!"

Loaded down, Millicent used her forehead to knock on Brianna's door.

The door flung open. "What!" Brianna was her usual self.

"I brought our favorites up so we can eat together in peace and quiet." Millicent's voice reeked of need for acceptance that overpowered the flavorful Asian spices.

"I thought you didn't allow food in the bedrooms."

Brianna took a bowl of sesame chicken from Millicent's hand and headed downstairs. Millicent, feeling dejected, went to her bedroom to eat alone.

WHEN IT ALL FALLS APART

Wednesday rolled in and Millicent rolled out of bed in compliance with her internal alarm. She silenced her clock to keep in line with the war of no words she declared on Brian. She had no intention of going through with a divorce. She did intend on fighting immaturity with immaturity by making Brian walk on eggshells until she was ready to have a conversation.

Millicent added a twist to her ordinary morning routine. Instead of ordering everyone down to the table, she made herself breakfast, cleaned and put away the dishes. She left cereal, a bowl of fruit, and a couple of nutrition bars on the table as a quick option for whoever bothered to venture downstairs for brunch, lunch or an early dinner. Satisfied with her spousal and parental due diligence, Millicent left for work.

****

It was game day for the veteran MVP. Millicent's face showed no sign of mercy as she strutted off the elevator in her baby blue power suit ready to schmooze, serve and seal the deal that would solidify her fate as next at the helm. She entered her office and sat down in her desk chair, before she could verbalize her relaxation, Pamela walked in.

"Who did you decide would take the house?" Pamela settled down into her imprint in the chair in front of Millicent's desk. "If I were you, I would consider condo living. There is this cute community seconds away from me and they have a two bedroom available. I assume you and Pinwheel will be the only ones staying there unless you plan on her living with Brian. I wouldn't blame you. Trust me, being a single mother is hard, but this will be fun."

"Pamela, shut up. I'm not divorcing Brian. My family will remain intact but thank you for your concern."

Pamela took the hint. "Well, excuse me. I guess I'll go back to my desk and wait until I'm needed."

"Yeah, you do that." Millicent remembered something, "Where are the samples? I want to get the room set up for the presentation."

Pamela turned around and released the lump in her throat. "Millicent—"

"Pamela, don't do this to me." Pamela using Millicent's government name was never a good sign. Millicent stood up, readying herself for the worse. "Pamela, I'm not in the mood for jokes."

"Millicent, when I left yesterday, I went to pick up Keisha. The sitter advised she was running a fever, so I stopped by the pharmacy. After that, I went home to take care of her. I completely forgot about the samples."

Millicent stumbled backwards into her seat. She refused to hear another one of Pamela's excuses and slid her chair to the phone to dial Chris. She checked the time and prayed he would answer. "Hey Chris, this is Millicent Hamilton. Yes, my assistant forgot to pick them up yesterday." Out the corner of her eye she saw Pamela storm out of her office as if she had a reason to be upset. "Chris, I really need to get those samples. I have a very important meeting this morning. It's ten till nine, I can be there in maybe twenty minutes. Oh great Chris, you're a lifesaver! See you in a few."

Millicent gathered her purse and keys and raced out the door for the elevator. She heard Pamela in the background. "Keisha feels better, thanks for asking!"

****

Traffic couldn't move fast enough for Millicent as she sped down the street, weaving in between vehicles as if she was driving an obstacle course.

"Come on truck, get out of my way! Why are you honking at me, stupid? You're the one driving like an old lady," Millicent hurled insults as she honked back. "Go! Go! Go! Move it people!" She clocked fifty in a thirty-five and rolled through stop signs and red lights. If a cop pulled her over, it would be a high-speed chase to Chris' shop and back to work. Nothing was stopping her from getting those samples back in time for the meeting.

Millicent's brakes screeched outside of Chris' studio fifteen minutes on the dot. Chris lived a couple of blocks away and as Millicent pulled up, he was parking his car. There was no time to search for an empty space; instead, Millicent parked in front of the store. The traffic resembled a professional speedway now. On the shop's narrow street, it was impossible for Millicent to exit her vehicle. She rolled down her passenger window and instructed Chris to bring the samples to the car.

Chris gave a thumbs-up and responded, "No problem, Mrs. Hamilton."

"Where are you Chris?" Millicent's heart skipped a beat with every tick coming from her watch. Once Chris reemerged with the samples, her normal rhythm returned. Crisis avoided and Millicent had enough time to return to work and prep the presentation room, assuming her clients weren't early. To be safe, she needed to contact Ryan and ask him to stall the clients if they arrived before her.

"Do you want these in the backseat, Mrs. Hamilton?"

"Yes please, Chris." Millicent used her car's call feature, "Dial Ryan." The phone rang.

"Mrs. Hamilton, the door won't open."

"That door can be a little tricky." *Another honey-do task my honey failed to do.* "Let me help you with that."

Without hesitation, Millicent unfastened her seat belt and opened the driver's side door. What followed were chords of brakes screeching and an accordion solo of metal crushing metal with a crescendo of glass breaking filling the humid, morning air.

"Oh my God, Mrs. Hamilton!"

"Hello," Ryan's voice traveled through the car's speakers.

"Someone call 9-1-1," Chris commanded the gathering crowd.

"I couldn't see her. I'm innocent! It was an accident," the driver of the delivery truck confessed as he approached the scene of impact for further investigation.

Ryan listened to the commotion. "What's going on? Who's there?"

Chris answered, "Mrs. Hamilton was hit!"

****

At the Hamilton home, action was on suspension until Brianna broke the rules of the silent game. "Dad, is your wife coming back home to fix us breakfast? This is the second day in a row. Nana was right, you need to put her in check or get in the kitchen and make something happen. I'm sure your food couldn't be any worse," Brianna barked at her father with her hands on her hips. Her little sister posed at her side in the same threatening manner. The girls stood in front of their father as he sat on the couch with his cell phone up to his ear.

Brian didn't say anything. He was preoccupied with attempting to reach Millicent to put an end to the divorce talk but was unsuccessful.

"Dad," Brianna yelled and snapped her fingers at her

father like a trainer trying to get a puppy to perform a trick for a treat.

Brian stayed mum and listened to Millicent's voicemail for the tenth time. It wasn't until simultaneous knocking and ringing at the front door brought him out of his daze, he wasn't in a playful mood. "Is it that serious?" Brian tossed his cell phone on the couch, pushed past his daughters as they stomped their way back upstairs to their rooms and made his way to the front door to confront the impatient visitor. "Can I help you?" He was unaware of the surprise waiting on the other side.

"Yes, you can bring in my bags, Son," Valerie said.

"Mom, I wasn't expecting you." Brian gave his mother a kiss on the cheek as she entered the house.

"My flight arrived early. I decided to catch a cab instead of waiting for someone to pick me up."

Brian gathered his mother's luggage and carried them to the guest room. This granted Valerie a break to perform an impromptu inspection. She started rubbing her fingers across bookshelves and figurines. Next, she proceeded to spank pillows and shook curtains like unruly children, all in an effort to uncover any amount of dust. She found nothing but an out of place toy unicorn. Brian returned before she could make her way into the kitchen to check for crumbs, water spots, expired food or any evidence to prove Millicent was an unfit homemaker.

"Mom, can I get you anything?"

"I was expecting breakfast to settle my stomach. I guess your wife didn't have time to prepare anything before she ran off to work this morning."

"Actually Mom," Brian thought of a quick lie. "I was planning on taking you and the girls out for breakfast. Girls, Nana's here lets go eat!"

"Brian, don't you get tired of eating out every day? When are you going to put your foot down and demand more support from that wife of yours? Do I need to do it for you?"

Brian looked into his mother's eyes and pleaded for her safety. "Mom, whatever you do, don't mention support around Millicent."

"Honey, if you think I'm going to bite my tongue in front of Mrs. Almighty, you know nothing about me."

"Mom, please behave. She's my wife."

"First mistake, second was quitting your job. I tell you if I hear or receive another newspaper or magazine clipping from another one of my league members about my famous daughter-in-law, I'm going to have a fit. I raised you to be head of the household, not Mr. Mom. If I'm not mistaken, I'm the only living Mrs. Hamilton. She's legally Millicent Tyler-Hamilton, correct?"

"We've discussed this before, once when we got married and again when Penny was born. Millicent kept Tyler out of respect for her father's legacy since she was the only child. Anyway, she goes by Millicent Hamilton."

"Exactly, goes by, but how does she feel? Are you sure she's going to be here for you and the girls as long as you both shall live; or, is she too busy living this celebrity lifestyle to notice you all even exist? I've heard about those high-powered, professional men that she's socializing with in pictures. What makes you think she won't bite into one of those apples? Maybe she already has. It would be easy for her to erase that hyphen Hamilton from her and Penny's name and leave you and Bri behind. How would you behave then?"

It seemed Valerie had some clairvoyant ability, or a sick sense for drama. Despite all that happened the last two days, Brian had no evidence that his wife was ever unfaithful. Millicent throwing around divorce was another example of them showing who could hit back the hardest. They both needed a time-out from the bickering, but divorce was an option neither one would ever concede to.

"Mom, you really have no clue."

"No? Well enlighten me, Son."

"Nana!" The kids made their way into the living room.

"Hello my angels, you both have gotten so big."

"Great, let's go eat ladies so you can all get reacquainted." Brian rushed his family toward the garage to end the conversation between him and Valerie. He could only tackle one woman upset with him at a time. At this moment, Millicent was the bigger issue on his plate. Silent treatment or not, he had to make things right with her. Valerie's topic would come up again. Hopefully, it would occur over the phone after she made it back to Thomasville.

The family didn't make it past the mudroom when the telephone rang.

"You want me to get that," Brianna asked.

"No," Brian rebuffed, "I'm sure it's not important. Let it go to voicemail."

Everyone climbed into the SUV and fastened their seat belt. Brian backed out of the garage and onto the driveway. While waiting for the door to close, his cell phone began to vibrate and caused all passengers to look down at the center console.

"Answer it now, not when we get on the road," cautioned Valerie.

Brian, the obedient son, shifted the gear from R to P and answered his phone, "Hello, this is Brian." After his greeting, there was a long pause but the change in Brian's facial expression gave away the ending. He disconnected from the caller and shifted the vehicle in reverse.

"Son, what's wrong?"

Brian peered in the rear view mirror fixated on Brianna and the obstacles he thought were long behind him.

"Brian," Valerie called to her son.

Brian answered, "We have to get to the hospital."

A CHANGE IS COMING

A gust of wind caused a discarded flyer to brush across Millicent's legs, but that had no affect in her awakening. It was the fumes of asphalt and leaked engine oil that made her open her eyes for what seemed like the first time. She laid face up in the middle of the street staring into the heavens. Heavy, ominous clouds appeared to struggle for position in the sky as they fell over each other. The escaping rays started to heat her like an egg in a frying pan.

What happened?

Millicent's body throbbed as if a cannon blasted her onto the street. Gritty pieces of pavement pushed into the flesh of her hands and feet as she got up from the ground and made her way to the sidewalk of a strip mall. She examined herself in a storefront window. Pirouetting around like a jewelry box ballerina, Millicent didn't see any signs of injuries. Even the tailored, blue suit that covered her five feet, five inches frame was without any tears or stains. Glass peppered her hair's dark brown ringlets. She reached out her arms and wiggled her fingers. She looked down at her lower extremities and did the same with her toes. Everything was in proper working order. With the exception of being barefoot in public, she looked fine, but something was very wrong. Millicent had no idea what events led her to the place where she stood or who the woman was staring back at her.

Looking in the window, Millicent saw red and blue flashes highlighting a growing audience behind her. She walked toward the crowd in hopes to find an answer to her identity or, at least, an answer to what happened before her eyes opened. The more Millicent progressed, the further the crowd seemed before it vanished. Her view substituted with rapid moving, strategically placed black shapes until darkness surrounded her. Fear of the unknown caused Millicent to panic, her instincts triggered her to run with no specific location in mind other than out. Her feet dictated her body's course. She stopped for air, and a crowd of indistinct people surrounded all sides of her. A small child came into focus.

"Why are you running," the boy questioned. "You don't have to run. He's only going to take you when it's your time anyway."

"Take me where? Where are we," Millicent asked.

The small boy blended into the crowd without offering any answers. Millicent pushed her way in and out of the gathering to look for the child when a hypnotizing, bright spotlight diverted her attention. Millicent no longer felt the warmth of the ground underneath her feet as the light lifted her closer to its base.

****

"Does anyone know the name of the patient or what happened," EMT One solicited the crowd for an answer.

Chris replied first, "Her name is Millicent Hamilton."

The driver of the truck that struck Millicent answered second, "Some crazy birds flew into my windshield. It was an accident. I didn't hit her on purpose. Is she going to make it?"

"She has a slight pulse which is a good sign. Her strength will determine the rest," EMT Two responded as he and his partner hoisted Millicent into the back of the ambulance and connected her to their machines to stabilize her condition.

"What hospital are you taking her to," Chris inquired.

"Calverton Memorial," EMT Two specified.

Calverton Memorial was the oldest hospital in Calverton. Age and outer appearance didn't negate the fact that it's recruited some of the best physicians in the world. It topped lists as the best hospital in the southeast region due to its technological advancements and medical research on multiple occasions. Millicent would receive exceptional, quality care.

"Her BP's dropping we need to get her out of here quick. Stay with us Mrs. Millicent Hamilton. You got to fight!" EMT One exited the back of the ambulance, closed the doors behind him and returned to the driver's seat. The engine revved up with the siren blasting as they zigzagged through traffic en route to the hospital.

****

"I guess now's my time?" Millicent didn't know what led her to her current reality; nonetheless, she figured out what was ahead. "Do I have to go? Is there someone up there? Answer me!"

"Don't go into the light," a distorted voice exclaimed.

"I don't think I have any other options. It's pulling me, not the other way around."

The distorted voice returned, "You trust what's on the other side? Are you that sure of your fate? There's always a Plan B or do you not want a second chance? Listen, if you don't want to go, you don't have to. What's it going to be?"

"I don't want to go," Millicent proclaimed.

In that instant, a strong force overpowered Millicent's body and pushed her out of the light's path. The impact jolted her back to earth. Her surroundings morphed like drawings in a flip-book as she voyaged through different periods of black to white to color. She eventually glided to the ground like a paper plane.

"Look out!" That same voice and force moved her out of the way of a runaway emergency vehicle, and she stumbled back onto the sidewalk. "You're going to have to learn to be more careful if you plan on keeping all your feathers."

"I don't know what the heck is going on, but I really think I need a doctor." Millicent turned around to face the pushy Good Samaritan only to catch a glimpse of them flying away. Shocked and confused by her discovery, "You're a bird!"

Beyond her sight of recognition, the bird replied, "So are you."

Millicent turned to look into the same store window as before but her image had drastically changed.

IT'S NOT OK

Everything moved in slow motion. Walking down the halls of Calverton Memorial Hospital was all too familiar to Brian. The strong stench of disinfectant conquered the agony and smell of death. It brought back memories from roughly nine years ago when his first wife checked in to give birth to their second child. It was a high-risk pregnancy with major complications during delivery. Neither she nor the baby survived which affected Brian in an unusual way. Not one to follow rules, he went directly to the last stage of grief—acceptance. On what started as one of the happiest days of his life, Brian returned home alone. He packed up his wife's belongings along with the nursery and locked everything away, mentally and physically, in the attic. He simply moved on and reconnected with his childhood sweetheart, now second wife.

"The patient's name is Millicent Hamilton, I'm her husband," Brian informed the administrator on duty.

"Yes, Mrs. Millicent Hamilton was brought in a while ago sustaining…." The receptionist spared the details of Millicent's condition as Brianna and Penny made their presence known. "She is currently in the OR. Take the elevator to the third floor. The waiting area will be on the left. I'll let the doctor know the family is here."

****

The family exited the elevator on the third floor. Ryan greeted them as they entered the waiting area. He pulled Brian and Valerie to the side, away from the youthful ears, and recounted his second hand understanding of what happened. Brianna and Penny rested their bottoms in the faux leather chairs. Penny picked up a children's book and thumbed through the colorful pages seemingly unaware of the seriousness of their trip to the hospital. Brianna chose the closest magazine within her reach, opened it up, and held it close to her face. She wasn't interested in the cover story on the economic crisis of America; instead, Brianna used it as a shield to prevent anyone from seeing her crying.

This trip to the hospital triggered pent up emotions for Brianna of the day her mother and baby brother left to be with God. She remembered waiting with anticipation for her expanded family to walk through the door. Although she was very clear on not going near any poop-filled diapers, Brianna couldn't wait to hold, feed and dote on the newborn. It was her intention to be the best big sister; sadly, she only saw her father cross the threshold in an emotionless state.

Brian passed the beaming expressions on Brianna and Valerie's faces and went up the stairs to the bedroom he transformed into a nursery with the help of his daughter. The room contained all things fit for a little prince including a cloud border and walls littered with family photos. Valerie followed behind Brian but soon returned downstairs with a ruined face to tell her grandchild that her mother and brother were now living amongst the sun, moon and stars. Brianna's juvenile heart only comprehended her mom left without saying goodbye and that she loved her as she did on other occasions when she would be away from her baby girl. That pain stayed.

"Bri, Penny, I want you to go with Nana and Chris to get something to eat, after that Chris will take you all home." Brian received a nod of approval from three of the four recipients of his message.

Brianna removed her protective shield, rose from her seat and made her intentions known with a bold statement. "I'm not going anywhere!"

Ryan stepped into the conversation, "Hey guys, I think you all need to be here for Millicent. I'm going to head back to work. Brian, keep me posted and let me know if you need anything. I'll be praying for you all."

The family thanked Ryan as he departed.

Valerie approached her oldest grandchild and stroked her hair in an effort to calm the upset teen, "Bri, everything is going to be OK."

That statement was another trigger of deep-seated rage within Brianna. She flicked her grandmother's hand and walked to the opposite side, ready for round one. "OK, like the last time Nana? You told me the same thing when I was six. Mom and the baby are in heaven and everything is going to be OK. You lied to me! Everything changed and nobody cared. Nobody cared about me. I lost my mother, and no one bothered to find out how it affected me. You went back home to Thomasville. You hardly ever call or visit." Brianna pointed her finger like the barrel of a gun at Brian. "And you packed up their stuff and hid it in the attic as if they never existed. I'd sneak up there every night when I was little to play in my mother's things." Brianna paced back and forth and shed the memories from her past with every step. "I smelled her perfumes and tried to remember which scent she wore the most. I put on her lipstick, and kissed the palms of my hands like the kisses she gave me. She started doing that my first day of kindergarten. With all those kids, I asked, 'What if they don't like me?' She kneeled down, left her mark in my hands and assured me if I ever felt sad and lonely, all I had to do was open my hands and know I had someone who would always be there to give me lots of love and kisses. I didn't want to wash my hands at all that day until our palms touched again.

The adults listening to the verbal debut of Brianna's anguish felt their hearts crack.

Nostalgia turned back to anger as Brianna continued. "But that was a lie too because she's not here. You all abandoned me! I had no one to talk to, no one who would grieve with me." Brianna forced her anger back on Brian. "The only time you even mention them is on their birthdays and Mother's Day when we go to place flowers on their graves. You never even cried at the funeral. Why would you," Brianna's voice regressed from passion-laced to sarcasm, "a couple of years later you handed me a brand new mom. A year after that, I finally got the sibling I was promised. I guess in your adult minds that made everything better, but it wasn't. I've hated Millicent ever since she stole my mother's life.

The cracking continued while Brianna finished.

"Even though Millicent tried to be there and treat me like her own, I wasn't going to let her take over as my mother. I tried to make every moment of her life as crummy as possible because that's how I felt inside. I'm even jealous of my own sister." Brianna's attention turned to Penny. "Why did she have a mom and I didn't? What was so special about her lucky Penny?" Brianna reserved the last of her honesty for the adults. "I had this anger inside me my whole life and nobody seemed to care. Last night, when Millicent called the only memories I have of them crap I wanted her to die. I knew it was wrong when I wished it, and I feel horrible for saying it. I'll probably never get the chance to say I'm sorry for everything." Brianna pulled in her tears to insure her vow was coherent. "The only thing I can do now is make sure what happened to me doesn't happen to my little sister. She won't be alone, and she's not going to make the same mistakes I've made. I won't let her fill her emptiness with anger and do stupid stuff to erase the hurt. So, I'm not leaving until I know for myself what's happening with Millicent. If it does turn out to be the worst, I'll be there for Penny because I know her dad and grandmother won't be," Brianna sat back down in her chair, her tears on full display.

Heartbroken, Valerie and Brian both go to comfort Brianna. Their good intentions couldn't vanquish the teen's anger. Brianna's breaking point was in the making for years and wouldn't be resolved in a day especially not without a proper solution. Valerie and Brian sat down with the girls and waited.

Minutes turned into hours. Doctors and nurses walked by, none knew of Millicent's condition. Families came and went, leaving the Hamiltons to wait by themselves. At the start of the sixth hour, a doctor appeared in the waiting area.

"Hi, I'm Dr. Jones. Are you the family of Mrs. Millicent Hamilton," the doctor addressed the group.

"Millicent Tyler-Hamilton," Valerie took the liberty of correcting the doctor.

"He was right the first time, Ma," Brian responded to his mother before addressing the doctor, "Hello, I'm Brian, her husband." He approached the physician. Valerie clutched the girls at her side and shadowed Brian. All were prepared to hear the bad news.

Penny calmly left Valerie's side, positioned herself as head of the others, and asked the question everyone wanted answered, "Doctor, is my mommy in heaven?"

Looking down at Penny, the doctor replied, "No little one, your mother is not in heaven." Everyone exhaled a sigh of relief. The doctor looked back up at the adults. "It was touch and go for a moment. There were multiple fractures, facial lacerations, some internal bleeding which we were able to stop, and she suffered a serious contusion on her brain."

"When can we see her," Brianna asked.

"Well she is out of surgery, but—"

"When can she come home," Brianna interrupted the doctor.

Before the doctor had a chance to answer Brianna, Brian rattled off questions of his own, "Is she mobile? Like are her arms and legs working, or is she in a wheelchair? How am I going to get a wheelchair up the stairs? Will she need an in-home nurse?"

Feeling ignored, Valerie joined in, "How much is all this costing? Does she have insurance? I saw her pictured with the board members of this hospital; will all this be free of charge?"

Brianna, feeling overshadowed, repeated her questions getting louder with each repetition.

Overwhelmed by the barrage of inquiries, Dr. Jones barely noticed Penny tugging on his lab coat. She beckoned him to come down to her level. As the room quieted, Dr. Jones kneeled down to hear what Penny had to say.

"Is Mommy sleeping?"

"Yes Sweetheart, your mom is in a very deep sleep." Dr. Jones returned to his upright position to address the rest of the family. "She's in a coma. There is brain activity but I can't say if she will regain consciousness in a couple of hours, a couple of days or months. I can show you to her room; although, I don't think it's a good idea for everyone to be present." The doctor looked down at Penny. "At least not until you have a chance to explain Mrs. Hamilton's condition."

"Mrs. Tyler-Hamilton," Valerie chimed in.

"Mom, that's enough."

"Son, I'll stay out here with Penny. You and Bri should go in."

Brian agreed. He wrapped his arm around Brianna's

shoulder as they both followed the doctor beyond the double doors.

****

Dr. Jones led Brianna and Brian down the hall then around the corner to room three thirteen before he parted ways. Brian inhaled a deep breath of ammonia rich air as he looked at his daughter who was staring back at him. He entwined his right hand with Brianna's left and tightened his grip. Together, they turned the door handle.

Father and daughter walked in and saw Millicent with a bandaged head and face and all but her left arm in a cast. Brian dropped Brianna's hand and walked straight to Millicent's bedside. He pulled up and occupied an empty chair, cuffed her hand with his and cried.

Brianna walked through the sterile room to the other side of the bed and examined her stepmother's body as if she was a physician on her first day of residency. She felt the texture of the cast, gently pinched Millicent's toes then her fingers to make sure the white under her nail beds turned back to red. She spotted the tubes attached to Millicent's body and traced them back to the IV drip and beeping monitors. Her eyes followed the cords to make sure they plugged into an outlet. She went into her purse, retrieved her compact, held the mirror to Millicent's nose to see if it fogged up then stashed it back before her father looked up. She was satisfied that this wasn't grownups telling her what she wanted to hear. Millicent was still alive.

"Dad, we need to put some color and energy into this room, like pictures from home, her favorite blanket, flowers, and balloons." Brianna went over to the window and drew the blinds, "We also need to get some fresh air in here." Brianna attempted to open the window, "Dad, help me with the window...Dad...Dad!" Through the smudged pane of glass, Brianna saw her father in a different light. He was by Millicent's side with his head low, caressing her hand. A single tear arose and fell down the plotted path on Brianna's cheek. "Did you love her? Dad, did you love my mother?"

Brian, with matching tear trails, broke his prayer pose to answer his daughter. "How could you ask a question like that?"

"Look at your face! I've never seen you shed one tear since my mom died. You never cry. You're holding Millicent's hand and praying. I bet you didn't do that when they pronounced my mother dead. Did you even stick around to see if my little brother had your nose or my mother's long toes?" Brianna fought off crying as she conversed with her father. "Nana insisted that Millicent always had her claws in you. You rode your bikes together in grade school. She was your high school sweetheart. You two broke up when she decided to go out of state for college and you went to Thomasville Community College where you met my mom and settled. You never cared about her or me." Brianna turned her back on her father and stared out the window.

Brian released Millicent's hand. "Bri, I loved your mother. I never settled for her. When Millicent went to school out of state, it tore me to pieces. Your mother and I found each other, and she put me back together again. We met at a rally on campus. She needed volunteers to help at the food pantry. Your mother was always willing to help anyone. She was so full of life and optimism despite her upbringing. You see, she grew up in foster care."

"Foster care, where were her parents?" Intrigued by a never before mentioned detail of her mother's history yet unwilling to face her father, Brianna looked to his reflection in the window for an answer.

"She never knew her real parents. Her birth mother gave her up for adoption when she was born and she never found a permanent home. She endured some hard times while in the system, but she never let her past define or limit her. That's what made me fall in love with her. I admired her strength. She always wanted a family of her own to love and be loved unconditionally." Archived thoughts of his lost love played in his head and left Brian with delight on his face. "She really was the perfect wife, daughter-in-law and mother. When you were born, she would always say you were her window."

"Her window, what does that mean?" Brianna turned to her father's real image.

"It's from a locket she wore. She received it as a gift when she was younger. Instead of the typical photo inside, she kept a piece of paper with an inscription on it. What did it say? It was some kind of affirmation, something along the lines of a closed door equals a window or something like that. Her favorite foster mother recited it to her to help her cope through the tough days. The locket was the first thing I rummaged for when I came home that day. We were in such a hurry that morning she forgot to put it on. She begged me to turn around and get it. It was her good luck charm. I, of course, thought she was being ridiculous and stayed on track to the hospital. I guess I forgot the significance of both." Brian joined Brianna by the window. "When your mother died it was the first time I was ever confronted with death. My father died when I was still in the womb and my grandparents died years before that. I didn't know how to process it all. I felt crushed on the inside and all I could think about was how I was going to raise you alone. When Millicent came back into my life it was strictly for moral support, but the more time we spent together the more our flame started to rekindle. I thought it was God answering my prayers."

Brianna rolled her eyes at the response her dad gave. "Answer to your prayers?" She returned to her outside view in her signature stance with arms folded. "What prayer was that, please God get rid of my wife and bring my true love back to me?"

"Bri, you know that's not what I meant," Brian forced Brianna to face him. "I know now the way I handled Mari and the baby's death was wrong, I take responsibility for that. I'm sorry I never shared stories of how amazing she was. That is my fault and my fault alone. You can hate me for that if you want, but don't ever say I didn't love her because that's not true."

Brianna and Brian both turned and stared out the window like subjects for a still life painting.

Brianna broke her form to pose another question to her father, "Did you tell her you loved her? I mean, I've heard you tell Millicent once or twice, usually after you've screwed up though."

"I did, but not as much as I should have," Brian held his daughter in his arms, "I promise to share those words more often."

Brianna surrendered to her father. "Yeah, you should, and you can still tell me those stories about how amazing my mom was."

Brian kissed his daughter on the forehead and made a request, "Do me a favor, give me a couple of minutes before we go and get Nana and Penny?"

Brianna understood her father's need to be alone with Millicent. "Sure, Dad." She exited the room. The closed hospital door held her up as the faucets in her eyes turned on again. How would she get through another traumatic event? If only she could sulk and pout her way out of this or swipe it away with one of her playlists. The preaching of her stepmother and father of not maturing too fast finally stuck. Being an adult was hard, but one had to be in the Hamilton household full-time for the sake of the family, especially Penny.

On the other side of the door, Brian gazed out the window. It looked like rain earlier, but the clouds dissipated. The sun was on center stage. His eyes started low, weighted by the byproduct of his grief. With all the false promises he made throughout his marriage, Brian wasn't allowing anything to deny his chance of growing old with Millicent. Faith lifted his head and he looked to the sky and had a conversation with his wife. "Is this your way of teaching me a lesson Millicent? If this is some type of elaborate hoax, I swear I will never forgive you.

Brian looked at his wife expecting her to jump out of the hospital bed, rush to his side and apologize for going too far in trying to prove her point. That didn't happen. Saddened by the truth, he turned back to the window.

"Our eight year anniversary is in twelve days. I planned to gift you skimpy lingerie. Before you had a chance to go off on how sexist and selfish I was, I would reveal my real gift. I made reservations for a trip back to Jamaica. That's why Mom came to get the girls. I guilted her into keeping them for the summer. I even worked it out with your boss to let you take off for a long period on short notice. There was no need for me to rush any business planning. I wanted to work on our marriage. I know things between us are strained, and I know it's my fault. The firing was an unexpected blow to my ego. That, along with Bri's constant goofing off, wore me out. I always knew her rebellion was my fault too. I didn't want to own up to it, but I never imagined how far the damage went.

Brian turned back to Millicent to make a confession. "I'll admit I have a problem with properly loving the women in my life. I dropped the ball with Mari, and that screwed Bri up. I give my mother too much say. I didn't appreciate you as an equal and acting jealous over your male clients didn't help things. I know you would never disgrace our marriage. I also know I'm not the right pedigree for you. I'm not rich or influential. I pushed you away instead of dealing with my own issues. I think my reaction to Mari's death screwed me up too. I let my insecurities show and even rub off on you. I don't want to change you Millicent; I love you the way you are. I wanted to use this vacation as an opportunity for a fresh start. Air out everything and strengthen our relationship. I guess I waited too late. When you told me you wanted a divorce, I realized how much trouble I caused by neglecting you and your happiness. More importantly, I realized that there is no way I can live the life I want without you.

Brian returned to Millicent's side to complete his unmasking face to face. He took his wife's free hand and placed his right thumb and index finger on the lightened area of skin caused by her wedding band as if he was proposing all over again. "Our life is etched right here. From love, loss, back to love, we've survived it all. We've made missteps but never faded. You're going to recover from this. There is no way I'm losing my soul mate. Forever isn't up." Brian ended with a kiss on the lips of his bride.

I'M A WHAT

Millicent watched for what seemed like an eternity at her new image. The day's breeze passed over her five or six inches tall body covered in dull brown and gray feathers that replaced the ringlets of hair that cascaded past her shoulders. Her white polished toes transformed into scaly claws. She focused her beady eyes on her short, pointy beak. She didn't trust her vision. She reached out her wing and touched the tip. "Ouch!" It was real. Instead of a graceful pivot, Millicent teetered and stumbled for a side and back view. She reached out her left wing then her right, strummed her cloak of feathers back and forth like a harpsichordist. She shook her tail feathers, which attracted unwanted attention.

"Look, it's a bird," cheered a young boy who found interest in Millicent.

"Yes, now let's go inside, James," his mother replied.

"Do I have to? This is a woman's clothing store. I thought we were going to get me some new sneakers."

"Not until after I find a couple of outfits for our trip."

The boy whispered to Millicent, "I'm taking you with me." Before Millicent could object, he scooped her up by the throat and cradled her in his chubby hands as he followed his mother into the store.

Millicent bounced around in the boy's hands as he trailed his mom up and down the aisles of vibrant blouses and pants. That's when she saw it. On a faceless mannequin, was a carbon copy of the baby blue suit that covered Millicent's human body next to a sign that read reduced.

"Don't worry, I'll find plenty of worms for you to eat."

"James, who are you talking to?"

The boy stashed Millicent behind his back.

"What are you hiding," his mother demanded as she tried to uncover the secret.

"It's just a bird," the boy revealed while he presented Millicent like a gift to his mother.

"Put that thing down," his mom screamed, "birds are infested with bugs and diseases."

The mother smacked Millicent out of her son's hand and she landed on a neat stack of cotton shirts. More screams accompanied Millicent's crash landing. Another customer flung her to the ground. Her body swept away, not by a knight in shining armor, but by someone with a broom. She tumbled beak over feet out the door and back to the sidewalk where she started.

"Are you OK," another bird queried. Millicent was too transfixed on herself that she didn't notice she had company on the sidewalk. "My name is Anna, and you are?"

I'm a bird?

"Did you hear me? Can you talk?"

I'm a bird.

"Hello!"

How do I respond? "Tweet…tweet…tweet."

"You can't be serious," Anna asked then informed Millicent, "you don't have to say tweet you can talk normal like me."

She makes a good point. "I don't know my name, where I am or how I got here. The only thing I'm semi-certain of is I was in an accident and turned into this, but this isn't me. I'm not a bird. I'm a woman, medium height, curly brown hair, almond-shaped brown eyes and curves." As she spoke about her human features, Millicent pointed to the contrasting parts on her bird body, "What happened to the beautiful, black, woman with the cute toes? Where are my curves? Where's the human me? The one I saw in this same window before everything disappeared." Millicent looked around, "Everything's the same except me."

"I hate to be the one to break it to you, but it had to be a very serious accident because you're dead. So your hair, cute toes, and nut shaped eyes are probably splattered up and down the street somewhere."

Anna administered a forthright explanation Millicent wasn't ready to face, "I'm dead?" Millicent felt faint, "There's no way I can be dead." She pondered over all the achievements she had left to accomplish. "I mean, I have so much going…but what…I mean I'm only…." She couldn't recall a single actuality. "What am I saying I can't remember anything, but I can't be dead. I don't accept that!"

"The sooner you accept it," Anna stated, "the easier this life will be."

"Easy for you to say, but I know this life can't be mine," Millicent protested as she took in another full-frontal visualization of her body, "I die only to come back as a sparrow? I don't get it."

Anna suggested, "Would you prefer a pigeon? Anyway, you sealed this fate on your own."

"On my own," annoyed by the stranger's lack of sympathy, Millicent responded with attitude, "well why are you here?"

"Hey, I'm only trying to be friendly. That's why I approached you." Anna offered Millicent a proposition, "Seeing your predicament, I can help. You're obviously new to this world, I can take you somewhere safe where you can eat and live."

Skeptical, Millicent asked, "At what cost?"

"What do you mean?"

"What do you want in return? I know nothing in life, any life, is free." Millicent quoted.

Anna replied with laughter, "You're dead. What could you have that I would possibly want?" Anna made it hard for Millicent to deny another good point. "Listen, let me help you. No strings attached."

"Thanks, I guess." Millicent turned her inquisition on someone other than herself, "So did you die too or have you always lived as a sparrow?"

Anna hoped to dodge that question, "Yes, I am like you minus the amnesia."

"How long have you lived as a bird?"

"Too long, but enough with the questions and follow me because we need to get to a safe place."

Millicent could not put one foot in front of the other without stumbling. She flapped her wings in an attempt to let the wind carry her into the sky, nothing happened. She tried again, hopping and flapping vigorously with the result being her landing on her butt.

"I can use some help now, if you don't mind," Millicent pleaded.

Anna came to Millicent's aid, "First, no erratic wing flapping. Be strong and in control, at the same time show some grace. Let your movements flow up and down like this," Anna elevated herself in the air and flapped her wings while continuing her instructions, "up and down, up and down." Anna's body moved with each command she spoke. She reached a couple of feet in the air, maneuvered her body to the right then left and repeated as if she was outlining a winding river. "Turn in the direction of where you want to go," she yelled down to Millicent.

After showing off, Anna returned to the ground, "OK, now try with me."

Anna made flying look effortless. Millicent wasn't sure of her outcome. With Anna by her side, she hopped up, flapped and fell. She tried again, hopped, flapped and fell. The third time had to yield a better result. She hopped up, flapped, flapped again and fell back on her bottom. "What am I doing wrong," Millicent asked as her impatience grew.

Anna tried to give her confidence, "Nothing, it takes practice."

"I'm tired plus I'm getting concrete burns on my butt." Millicent gave up on the flying lesson and turned to a grinning Anna. Anna's smile made Millicent smile and wonder, "What's so funny?"

"You remind me of a baby learning to walk. I think I'll have to try a different approach with you." Anna pushed Millicent from behind and they both took flight well above the heights Anna reached. They traveled beyond the tops of the surrounding structures before they perched on top of a light post.

"Anna, what are you planning on doing?"

"I'm going to teach you how to fly." Without warning, Anna pushed Millicent off the post.

Millicent panicked. This caused all of Anna's training to rush out of her bird brain. She streaked down to the earth like a rock, seconds away from experiencing two deaths in one day. Millicent prepared for impact when Anna dived underneath her and carried her back to the top of the light post.

Anna shouted, "What are you doing?"

"What am I doing? Why would you push me when you know I can't fly?"

"But you didn't even try. How do you know whether you can or can't accomplish something if you don't at least try first?"

Before Millicent had a chance to continue their tiff, Anna shoved her off again. This time Millicent took Anna's words to heart and started flapping her wings up, down, up, down, slow, controlled, graceful.

"See you got it," Anna circled Millicent like a proud

parent, "It's windy out. You can glide without flapping to avoid overexerting yourself."

Millicent continued to carry out Anna's commands and felt at ease. "I'm doing it!"

"Yeah, you've got it. Now follow me," Anna said.

Anna led as the two soared through the sky flying in between buildings, over trees and under stoplights. She taught Millicent aerial maneuvers while plunging in and out of clouds. As they crossed a lake, in an attempt to make nice for almost killing her again, Anna dipped down, tickled the water's surface with the tips of her wings, and caused sprinkles to moisten Millicent's body. She also gave Millicent a literal crash course in landing but being on the ground underwhelmed Millicent now that she rode the wind. Too bad she had to die to experience it.

Anna decreased her pace. "We're approaching our destination."

They landed on the rooftop of a white, two-story home. From the rooftop, they made their way to the back patio area that was shaded by an ivy-covered pergola.

Millicent investigated her new surroundings, "What's so safe about this place?"

"No pets and they don't mind sharing their leftovers." Anna pecked at a morsel of white bread on the ground. "You better eat before the others get back."

"What others," Millicent managed to get that question out before she started to feast.

"This is community property," Anna mumbled with bread in her mouth, "There're five to ten of us that call this place home with another ten to fifteen that I've rescued who pass through from time to time."

"Of us, so they were once human too," Millicent assumed.

Anna confirmed, "Yes, but don't dwell on anyone's past."

"Why not," Millicent continued to pry.

"You ask a lot of questions." Anna was not thrilled with this part of Millicent's personality. "Don't do that either when you're around the others."

Millicent underwent de-evolution from woman to bird in a matter of minutes. It was natural for her to have questions. Anna was not going to deny her asking them.

"I'm not with them now. I'm with you, the one eager to help me." Millicent wanted to test the authenticity of Anna's kindness. "So, what's the big deal about discussing someone's past?"

"If you must know, these sparrows are stuck in the illusions of their old lives. They can't acknowledge the fact that part of them is over and there's no returning. I keep telling them the past is a deceptive anchor. You can carry the weight around lowering it in different memory banks for a momentary euphoric fix or let it weigh you down until you drown from memories you didn't think were that deep. In order for you to move on, you must move forward. Move beyond your loved ones, your work, your luxury home, your sport cars, all those things left behind to focus on your eternal life. Be confident in knowing that those you left in your human existence are going to be fine without you. The sooner you realize that you're not part of the living world anymore the better. It makes our decision and life in this world more tolerable."

"But how does that help me," Millicent asked in an effort to relate, "I can't even remember my past to forget it."

"Is it always going to be about you?" Anna uncovered another character trait of Millicent she detested. "I guess you're a very special sparrow."

"So are you like a Fixer or something? The one wise sparrow that figured this all out and is compelled to share this death changing advice with the multitude; hence, fixing their hereafter."

Anna took her purpose seriously. "I prefer Guide. I don't know everything, but I can help new spirits navigate this life."

Millicent hadn't caught the hint she was rubbing Anna the wrong way. "Well Guide, what makes you so special that you feel the need to help everyone? Leave it in the past seems simple enough for anyone to follow."

"Trust me, it's easier vocalized than acted upon. If you feel you can handle this world on your own, then by all means go off and do you, whoever that is." Anna gave Millicent an out she wished she would take.

Millicent needed help, but she couldn't turn off the interrogative mechanism in her brain. "Did you find the others like you found me?"

Anna had to think about the answer to that question. "A few made it here by themselves. I did find some of the others while I was out and brought them here. We can see it happening."

"See what," Millicent wondered.

"See the change from human to bird. Some sparrows are so obsessed you can catch them on top of buildings and houses or roosted on power lines like some macabre composition waiting to see if the newly dead will follow the light, or choose to leave and become one of us."

"Have you seen any stay with the light?" Millicent was curious.

"I've seen a couple of smart ones."

That remark puzzled Millicent. "Smart ones, so if you had to do it all over again you would've stayed with the light?"

"I didn't say that, I wouldn't change my decision."

"You're telling everyone else to forget and move on from their past, but have you?"

Anna hesitated before answering, "No, and I said it was

easier said than done, didn't I? Anyway, it's not my past that I'm trying to recapture, it's my future I'm trying to protect."

Millicent's confusion increased. It was clear Anna had a personal agenda and wasn't elaborating on the details. After Millicent digested her third piece of bread, she tried to change the subject. "We're talking sparrows who were once human. Are there any talking, former human blue jays, parrots or swans?" Millicent looked down at her tiny body and wished she had a say in her afterlife image.

"We only come in sparrow form. There's segregation in the bird community. I've encountered cardinals, robins and other species but they don't talk like you and me."

"Are there any other bird species we can communicate with?"

"I've heard the crows can, except I've given up on figuring them out. They're very peculiar and constantly watching us. I believe they act as our boundaries in this world, making sure we don't cause any more disruptions to His plan. We stay away from them; although, there's one sparrow who claims he talks with them all the time. He's as crazy as they come, be sure to stay away from him as well."

"Got it, I should stay away from the crows and the crazy sparrow." Bored with the rules and regulations, Millicent wanted to discover more about Anna's off-duty activities, "So what would be a typical day for you? I mean if you weren't here with me, what would you and the flock be doing?"

"I don't hang out with the flock." Anna fell for the bait and volunteered a slim insight into her sparrow life, "There was this one sparrow that I was close with before she disappeared. She was like the best friend I had in my human existence. You actually remind me of her a little, aside from your talkative nature. She came in with amnesia too. Her name was Sarah. It's just me and Gladys now."

"Who's Gladys?" Millicent indulged in her fourth crumb of bread. Her full line not reached, nor her question limit, "How long has she been part of the living dead?" Millicent's attempt to lighten the mood only amused her.

"What did I tell you about asking personal questions? You should listen more, talk less and stop with the wise cracks. In fact, it may be a good idea for you not to speak at all around the others. You should wait until you remember how to talk to people without being so condescending."

"Will do," Millicent sheepishly agreed. Anna's fit of anger caused Millicent to wonder if Anna died from an accident, natural causes or bludgeoned to death. In her hush moment, Millicent also imagined what her human life was like. Did loneliness and angst reside in her female form as well? She thought about what she was doing this morning, if she was at peace or upset, was she trying to avoid something, or what was so important that she was willing to die for and who's left mourning her. Nothing came into focus.

Finished with her breakfast, Millicent noticed the other sparrows returning. Anna approached one who must be Gladys. They looked similar but all the sparrows looked the same. There were subtle differences, some were heavier with darker feathers or other distinctive markings, but overall everyone looked alike. There was no distinction in age either. Anna carried a certain confidence and stood out from the others as a leader, making her easily identifiable. Gladys moved slower, which could be an indication that she was older. Although curiosity emerged in Millicent, Anna's stern warning made her keep her beak shut.

Millicent continued to observe Anna and Gladys as they talked. They suddenly looked in her direction. Millicent changed her point of view to avoid being the weird misfit waiting on acceptance into the popular girls club.

"She's new," a male's voice from above pointed out.

Before Millicent could lift her head, she was surrounded by sparrows who bombarded her with questions that linked to their past. Maybe Anna's teachings weren't as effective as she hoped.

"Hey, hush...be quiet...get away from her." Anna stampeded her way toward Millicent to help. "Back up, she's a Small."

A collective sigh echoed through the air as the sparrows went back to their resting places atop the pergola. Before Anna and Gladys could resume their private conversation, Millicent needed clarification. "Anna, what's a Small?"

"S-M-L, Spirit with Memory Loss," Anna replied before flying away with Gladys.

"Small!" The male voice that started the frenzy earlier landed in front of Millicent. He was a smaller built bird with black markings. His voice was loud and he had a serious lack of respect for personal space, which made Millicent uncomfortable. He had shifty eyes and gave off a tough guy vibe. He was scarred which signified a hard-fought survivor or a multi-occasion loser. "A couple of us are going for a bath. Do you want to come?"

The invitation sounded better than loitering around doing nothing, so she accepted, "Sure."

Millicent thought they would take a longer trip, like back to the lake she and Anna passed on their way to the house, but they ended up in what appeared to be the unfinished part of the side yard. The grass had faded away like the paint on the privacy fence that was no longer private due to the broken pickets. Lumber was there, but no one bothered to make the repairs. Millicent wondered what type of people occupied the residence.

"Where's the water." Millicent scoped the grounds for a

leaky faucet or puddle.

"You don't need water," the male sparrow retorted, "it's a dust bath."

Millicent's enthusiasm diminished like the grass and paint. "I think I'll pass."

"Don't be a prude, let the dirt get all in your feathers." The male sparrow and the others splashed in the dirt, this created clouds of dust and small indentions in the earth. They laughed and had a blast. Millicent didn't want to ostracize herself further than what Anna already accomplished, so she joined in.

"There you go." The male sparrow was thrilled he convinced the new girl to partake in their pastime. "See, it's not so bad."

"No, it's not." Millicent's comfort allowed her inquisitiveness to return. "I didn't get your name."

"I'm Samuel Rece, but everyone calls me Sammy." Sammy bowed in front of Millicent like a real gentleman. "You have no clue who you are, do you?"

"Not a clue," Millicent confirmed.

"There have been other sparrows that came in as Smalls but eventually they regained their memory, some quicker than others. Some stayed, others left," Sammy informed.

"Why did they leave, Sammy?"

"I'd assume to be around their loved ones or maybe they can't get past the nightmare of how they died."

"Why," Millicent had to question.

"All dead people don't die happy deaths," Sammy spoke. He set the scene. "Imagine realizing the woman you loved poisoning you for years while in cahoots with her lover, your physician, so they could kill you off and live happily ever after on your insurance money."

"Whoa Sammy, is that what happened to you?"

Sammy laughed at his far-fetched example. "No, that was from an episode of my favorite detective show. Man, I loved that show. A heart attack led to my demise eight years ago."

The sparkle in Sammy's eyes dimmed as he relapsed back to his human self. Millicent's solace converted to guilt for not practicing Anna's advice and making the one friendly sparrow relive his bad memories.

"Sammy, I know this is painful for you, but why don't you move on?"

"What are you talking about, Small? My memories are all I have. They're the real reason why any of us are even here. When the time came for me to leave the arms of my wife, two sons and daughter, I didn't want to go. I wanted to be there for them," Sammy looked down at his feathered chest, spread his wings and continued, "in any form. So I made the choice to stay here on earth and watch my wife celebrate our twenty-third anniversary alone, our twin sons go off to college and enter into manhood without me and my daughter go on her first date to the prom without me grilling the dude. I used to think it was worth it, until I later saw my family taken advantage of by Jeff, my best friend turned replacement. I can't bear to watch over them anymore. I guess this must be our punishment for not going when we were called."

"What is," Millicent asked.

"Coming back as sparrows." Sammy ditched his playful disposition. "How stupid were we to think we could out smart Him. We can see our loved ones but they don't give us a second glance. Sparrows are the runts of the bird species and look at these dull colors! They can't hear us speak. The living can only hear chirps. We can't hold them in our arms and comfort them. We can only shadow them like gnats. I guess we never should've stepped out of the light and accepted what was on the other side. I would've deserved it."

"We can still make the best of our life now." Millicent

wanted to offer a less dismal outlook, "Anna—"

"I see she's already gotten to you too. Anna, Anna, Anna, that's all I hear around this dreadful place. She's as lost as the rest of us. She puts on this saintly act, feeding these other idiots false hope, while she's still holding on to her past. You just met her, but she's nothing but a hypocrite." Sammy was so enraged he thought Anna was with him instead of Millicent. "Why don't you tell everyone the real reason you're here?"

"Why is she here, Sammy?" Millicent was dying to know.

"What?"

"Why is Anna here?"

"I don't know. Why are you asking me, Small?"

"Because you were saying—"

"I'm aware of what I said, Small! I said I didn't know, and I don't want to talk about what I was just talking about anymore. Did you hear that?"

"Yeah, I heard you." Listening to Sammy made Millicent understand two things. She should've trusted her initial instincts about him, and she never should've stepped out of the light.

One of Millicent's earliest recollections was of the blinding spotlight that lifted her in the air. Her eyes closed from the realness but reopened in shock as another fact surfaced. She didn't step out. She was convinced to leave, then pushed. Millicent had to figure out who persuaded her to go against her fate and why. Sammy had to be her inside man.

"Sammy, if I'm going to be tagging along with you, I have to be able to trust you. There's something you're not being straightforward with me regarding Anna. You can either tell me more about her or our developing friendship can begin and end right here, right now."

Sammy was reluctant at first but complied, "Follow

me." Before Sammy would give up any information, they journeyed to the end of the white picket fence in the rear of the property to avoid the consequence of having any part of their conversation make its way back to Anna. Despite Sammy's tough persona, it was clear that Anna had full run of the pergola and every bird that gathered there.

Sammy and Millicent landed on the upper support railing where he divulged what she wanted to hear, "Anna should've come back as a female dog, it would fit her personality better. Since I showed up here, she's been a rude, bossy, antisocial pain. She's a bully," Sammy wasn't shy with his words. "She doesn't want to help anyone. She only wants to keep us all under her command like some tyrant. The only one she wants to see happy is herself. Everyone here blindly obeys her. That is everyone except me."

"How did she get here?"

"Strangulation, blunt force trauma, a gunshot to the head, something gruesome I'm sure."

"Not how she died, how did she get to this house?"

"I was informed by some of the other birds that Gladys brought her here. From that point on, she's acted as if she owned the place."

"So Gladys is her Guide?"

"Her what," said Sammy.

"Guide, the one we can depend on to protect us in this world."

"First, Gladys is an old bird, she's been here longer than all of us, so she's not protecting anyone. B, we don't have Guides. You're born alone and you die alone. Dead people don't have guardian angels," Sammy snickered. "You may have someone look out for you but there's usually an ulterior motive behind it and you should watch your feathers."

Millicent tried to wrap her head around the new

information Sammy revealed. "I don't understand. Anna doesn't seem like a bad person, bossy yes, but she seems like she genuinely wants to help."

"Don't be so naïve. Listen kid, maybe she's trying to give you a helping of some of her false hope to make you feel safe while you regain your memory. Maybe she finally grew a heart, or maybe she really does like you and wants to be your friend," Sammy emphasized his last point in his best giggly, schoolgirl impression with cynicism wrapped around every word.

"Possibly. Sammy, what if I didn't decide on my own to step out of the light. What if another bird talked me into making that decision prior to pushing me out?"

Sammy's eyes doubled in size as they locked with Millicent's eyes. "It was Anna!"

"It could've been Anna." Millicent wasn't positive. "I didn't get a good look. Not that I would be able to tell that bird apart from Anna, you or any of the others around here."

"Do you remember anything about them, anything at all?"

"No, it was a brief run-in."

"What did they say to you?"

"I didn't have to go into the light if I didn't want to and that it was my choice."

"Somebody stole your peaceful ever after. You've got to find out what's going on and I'd start with Anna. If you're going to get anywhere with her, you have to be firm and direct. Let her know you're not playing games, or she'll walk all over you. You may not know who you are but I sense that warrior spirit in you," Sammy inflated Millicent's confidence like a coach prepping a bench warmer to make the game winning play. "Show no sign of feebleness, because you need the truth! Can you do that?"

"Yes, I can do it."

"Wonderful, let's go."

****

Sammy and Millicent returned to the house and found Anna and Gladys underneath the pergola. Millicent was nervous about the confrontation but grateful that Sammy would have her back. At least that's what she thought. She quickly learned Sammy wasn't a bird of his word when he veered off toward the side of the house back to his dust bath. Millicent would have to nix the idea of a good cop, bad cop routine and wing the interrogation solo.

As soon as Millicent's feet hit the cracked concrete, Anna's bossiness returned, "Where have you been," Anna addressed Millicent as if she was an hour past curfew.

"I was hanging out with Sammy," Millicent expressed.

"You were with Sammy," Anna asked, "as in Samuel Rece? What is he doing back here? Was Sarah with him?"

Anna's last question perplexed Millicent. "Who's Sarah?"

"My friend Sarah, the one I mentioned previously, Sammy's…Sammy is the sparrow I warned you earlier to stay away from."

"Why, is it because he's not afraid to stand up to you?" *He's not here so that may be a lie.*

"No, it's because nothing good could ever come from being around that psycho. Enough about Sammy, there's someone I'd like you to meet. Gladys, this is the Small I rescued this morning and decided to bring home."

Offended by Anna's smug introduction, Millicent sidestepped Gladys and rejected her advance of a cordial greeting. She focused her attention on her intended mark. "Anna we need to talk, alone!"

"Whatever you have to say to me you can say in front of Gladys."

Gladys complied with Millicent's wishes without resistance; however, Millicent wasn't satisfied. She wanted to convey that she too was an Alpha female like Sammy suggested. "No Gladys, Anna allowed you to stay so stay."

Anna butted up to Millicent, beak to beak, and made her displeasure for the verbal assault on Gladys known, "You will never speak to her like that ever again. Do I make myself clear?"

Millicent stuck to Sammy's advice and didn't back down. "So, it's acceptable for you to be a bossy, bully but no one else can?" Her statement resonated through the air, catching the attention of the other sparrows that caused them to abandon their activities and form a ring around her and Anna.

"Bird fight!" Sammy announced as everyone else squawked in approval.

The crowd brought unwanted pressure to Millicent. "Look Anna, I don't want to fight. I need to talk to you about why you pushed me earlier."

"I was trying to teach you how to fly."

"I mean before that, when you persuaded then pushed me out of the light. You took heaven away from me in exchange for feathers and a beak. I didn't ask for this."

"Fight! Fight! Fight!" Sammy hit all four corners of the pergola and encouraged the other sparrows to join in his chant.

"What are you rattling on about, Small?" Anna was annoyed at the spectacle Millicent incited and was prepared to end it by any means.

Gladys tried to defuse the situation and reached out her wing to pull Anna away.

"Stay out of this Gladys." Millicent continued her streak of bad decisions and pecked at Gladys' wing, "I'm talking to Anna now!"

All signs of a diplomatic resolution were void. Anna

swung her wing into Millicent's head and chest with the strength of a bull, not bird, and sent Millicent tumbling across the patio landing face first into a stone planter. Through intervals of blurry and clear vision, Millicent saw Anna approaching her with Gladys hopping in her path to cease any further altercations. Millicent blacked out.

THE BLAME GAME

Valerie and Penny sat together in the waiting area. It was quiet. No other bodies occupied the seats surrounding the grandmother and grandchild. With her head in Valerie's lap, Penny felt a slow drip of water hitting her forehead.

"Nana, why are you crying?"

Valerie fiddled with the barrettes in her youngest granddaughter's hair before she started her unfiltered monologue, "I'm very sad Penny. I see I haven't been the best grandmother to Bri. I left her when she needed me the most. I went back to Thomasville after the funeral as if everything was fine. I called every day for a while then once a week to see how she was doing in school. I congratulated her on band and dance recitals, but I never asked how she was emotionally. Once your mother married your father, I only called on birthdays and holidays. I should've known something was wrong when Bri was too busy to come to the phone and talk to me. The signs, all the classic signs, were right in my face. Even as a trained professional, I still couldn't see them. I was blind. Millicent blind-sided me when she slithered back and all I could see was her and rage. I deserted Bri. I stayed long enough to see her mother and my grandson placed in the ground. I left her in the care of Brian and some stranger. What spell Millicent has your father under I'll never figure out."

Penny knew the sound of grown folk's speech and reminded Valerie of her age with a question, "Nana, Mommy said you live in the country. Do you have unicorns?"

Valerie, trapped in her feelings, continued, "After she

broke his heart and enrolled in an out of state college, I thought my family finally cleansed itself of Ms. Millicent. Nope, she got a job in Calverton where Brian and Mari moved to start their family. When Mari died, to no surprise, Ms. Millicent started coming around to give her condolences to Brian. After that, she moved in. She and Brian eventually got married, and she's pulled his strings ever since. How could Brian possibly think Millicent would make a good wife, let alone stepmother? She doesn't have the qualities. She can't even comb your hair. Look how crooked these parts are." Valerie lifted her granddaughter's head, inspected her hairstyle and rested Penny's head back in her lap.

"You're cold Nana," Penny responded to her grandmother's hands on her cheeks.

"The only thing that interests your mother is her job and how ironic for her to be in a coma because of it. Well, this will be a wake-up call for her to reset her priorities, if she wakes up. I hope that job of hers provides good health insurance because this stay is going to cost a fortune. I bet you then she'll wish she hadn't made Brian quit his job."

Unable to withstand the disrespect, Penny leaped to her feet in defense of her mother and declared, "Daddy did my hair again this morning because he keeps stressing Mommy out, and that's why it looks funny. You're being mean Nana. Mommy is hurt and you're being mean to her. I'm going to tell Daddy!"

As if Penny mouthed the magic word abracadabra, Brian appeared from beyond the double doors like a superhero with Brianna behind him like a trusty sidekick.

Penny ran to her father. "Daddy, Nana is being mean," she sobbed as she latched on to his legs, which made him unable to move without her, "She said Mommy doesn't love us, only work, and that's why she's here. She said Mommy's not going to wake up."

"What on earth is going on out here," Brian expressed in disbelief. "Mom, did you tell her that?"

Valerie's righteous reputation was at stake, so she lied, "Brian, you know Penny has this wild imagination. All of this is too much for the poor child. She's making things up."

Being her mother's child, Penny wouldn't let Valerie get away with being dishonest. "Fibber," she yelled. Penny let go of her father to confront her grandmother with the same finger pointing as her older sister, "You did say that Nana! You said my mom is a witch and couldn't wait until Bri's mom died so she could pull my daddy's puppet strings. You said you don't visit as much because Bri made a dessert you didn't like." Penny walked back to her father and looked up at him as she finished the rest of her account, "Daddy, she also said you can't part my hair straight and you should shave it all off like my friend Eli. One more last thing Daddy, she said we're going to go broke when Mommy dies because all of our money will go to paying Mommy's sick bills, and you won't be working to make more money for us." Penny reattached herself to her father's knee and pleaded, "Don't leave me alone with her again, please Daddy!"

Brian and Brianna deciphered through the exaggerations in Penny's story to find the truth of what really happened and were flabbergasted.

"Nana," Brianna exclaimed.

"Mom," Brian snapped.

Valerie, stunned at the comprehension and attention span of a five-year-old, tried to explain, "Well, I...I didn't...yes I...but I," she couldn't find the words.

"Nana, how could you say that to her?"

"Yes...yes, I verbalized my concerns, but it was because of you, Honey." Valerie held Brianna's hands in hers as she explained, "Bri, I never realized how much pain you had in your heart until today. I'm hurting because I know the pain is partly my fault. I shouldn't have left you here to figure things out on your own. I didn't know that your father would neglect you too, but I do know that was solely due to Millicent and my son's insistent need to make that woman his only responsibility.

Valerie switched her attention to Brian and her angry grandmother attitude returned as she resumed, "Ever since you two were small, I've seen her dig her nails into you deep. She had you by the balls, following her around like a puppy dog since kindergarten. You pined over her for years even after she rejected you and you married Mari— the wife you really deserved. After her death, Millicent couldn't wait to weasel her way back into your life to continue controlling you.

Valerie's attention went back to Brianna along with her softer speaking voice as she concluded, "She didn't care about comforting your grieving child, continuing the brownie days, the dress up games or the surprise shopping trips that Bri used to do with Mari." Valerie transitioned back to Brian. "From what you complain to me about, Millicent doesn't even know how to cook. She does know how to gallivant around town with all these professional men, smiling for every camera in sight, disrespecting you while you're at home combing Penny's hair. Like snap out of it, she even made you quit your—"

"I got laid off," Brian roared. He grew out of the docile son and stepped into his mother's personal space to vent, "You can blame my boss, the economy, the president but you can't put that on Millicent. How dare you force your hatred for her on our kids. Millicent has done nothing but give unconditional love to Bri, Penny and me. She's laying in a hospital bed, fighting for her life and you have the audacity to degrade her when you never put forth an effort to get to know her. If you did, you would know that she works hard at her career, she also works hard to make our family work. She bites her tongue around you for the sake of me, the kids and your feelings when you obviously don't give a crap about hers."

"You always think she's so special," Valerie blurted.

"That's because she is," Brian corrected his mother, "God blessed me with two special women in my life, Mari and Millicent."

"Only two," Valerie fished for inclusion. "I guess me raising you all by myself doesn't make me special enough?"

"Telling a child her mother is a no-good manipulator doesn't make you special, it makes you evil." Brian headed toward the elevator. "Girls, we need to go home and pick up some of your mother's things and bring them back here." Brian extended an olive branch to Valerie in an attempt for her to make things right. "You can be a special part of this family Mom, but all negativity stops here and now or you can go back to Thomasville and not worry about seeing Millicent, me or the kids ever again."

Brian's wait for an answer wasn't lengthy. Without opening her mouth, Valerie showed her compliance by following behind the family as they stepped into the elevator.

****

The only thing brave enough to make a noise during the ride home was the vehicle's air conditioner. Brian kept his eyes on the road while Valerie, Brianna and Penny looked out their respective windows. When they arrived home, Brianna was the first to get out of the SUV. She entered the code on the outside keypad to allow her and Penny entry into the garage. From there, they entered the house. Valerie reached for the handle to open her door. Brian stopped her exit.

"Mom, how could you?"

Valerie stared at Brian as tears manifested in his eyes. She couldn't recall ever seeing him cry in her presence and thought that too was her doing. Valerie ransacked her brain for the right words to erase her mistake but failed in the recovery. The defeat caused her eyes to match Brian's eyes. Her second search came from her heart.

"I wanted to make things better, but I made them worse. I've always accused Millicent of turning you and the girls against me. Looks like I do a good job of that all by myself."

"Mom, I know how close you were to Mari, I loved her too, but she's gone. You and I both made detrimental decisions in how we handled her death. Listen, Millicent is still with us, and she's going to survive this. I need you to show her the same love you gave to Mari. Get rid of the notion that she is controlling me. She's not making me less of a man, if anything she inspires me to be a better one. She works an absurd amount of hours, yet still takes care of the house, the kids and me even when I don't reciprocate or appreciate it. We have our bad times, and yes, we argue but what married couple doesn't? The important thing is we make up because we love one another. I need you to understand, Millicent loves us all. She wasn't trying to take anything away, she wanted to add to our lives."

Valerie gave in, "OK, so she's perfect."

"No, she's not perfect. She's perfect for me."

Brian and Valerie exited the vehicle and entered the garage. Brian lagged behind to close the garage door while Valerie went inside. She saw Brianna gathering flowers, family pictures and some colorful knick-knacks on the kitchen table to use as decorations for Millicent's hospital room.

"Bri, have a seat," Valerie insisted, "I'd like to talk to

you."

Brianna sensed her grandmother's intentions and prevented the awkward moment. "Nana, I love you, but sometimes your words carry hurt and hate and they can be infectious. I know you mean well, I'm beginning to understand the actions of adults aren't always in the best interest for everyone involved. I get it, and I've already accepted your apology." In a kind gesture, Brianna patted her grandmother's back. "Penny is the one you need to sit down and convince that you're not a monster." Brianna gave Valerie a kiss on the cheek that signaled she forgave all things, past and present. She left Valerie to her task. "Penny's upstairs in her room."

Valerie walked to the bottom of the staircase. She was nervous and unsure how she would persuade Penny she wasn't a wicked grandma. She proceeded up the stairs, stopping briefly at each elevation. Before she reached the fourth step, Brian joined her.

"Mom, let's talk to Penny together."

Valerie nodded her head. She and Brian walked to Penny's door. They stopped just shy of the threshold.

"Who is she talking to," Valerie whispered to Brian.

Valerie and Brian lingered in front of the door and continued to eavesdrop on Penny.

HELP OR HINDRANCE

No remnants of war remained on the patio, only Sammy and Millicent. Some may downplay the event that occurred under the old pergola as a mere scrimmage, but Millicent was thankful to be alive in a sense. In her downtime, Millicent contemplated where her confrontation with Anna took a nasty turn. She settled on the moment she agreed to accompany Sammy to the dust bath.

"Small! Wake up," Sammy urged.

Millicent appeared oblivious. "What? Sammy, is that you?"

"Yes, get up," Sammy demanded.

"No," Millicent objected, "let me lay here."

"You can't. Now get up," Sammy insisted.

"Why not," Millicent asked. "Wait, is she still coming for me?" Millicent transformed from lackadaisical to frenzied. She twisted and turned, scraping her wings on the concrete to gain leverage to get to her feet.

"Calm down, shows over, everyone's gone," Sammy ensured.

"Yet you stayed. Is it because you," Millicent tried to replicate Sammy's school-girl voice, "want to be my friend?" Millicent entertained Sammy for a second then toughened her tone, "Or, do you just feel guilty since the altercation was your fault?"

Sammy was stunned. "My fault, I told you to be firm with Anna, not her mother."

"Her what," Millicent gasped.

"Oh, I didn't tell you Gladys is Anna's mother? Guess that's the one question you didn't ask, sorry." Sammy hid his giggle. He was gleeful someone took his advice and stood up to Anna, even happier it wasn't him, considering the outcome. "You absolutely can't stay here with the bad blood between you two. I can deliver a superior resting place."

Millicent's instincts were on burnt orange high alert, but she compromised her safe house with her irrationality. She had no other choice.

"Are you coming, Small?"

"Yes Sammy, I'm coming." *What have I gotten myself into?*

****

Millicent and Sammy drifted through the sky before arriving on the balcony of a brick townhouse. Millicent looked over the edge and saw the sidewalk occupied with joggers, dog walkers and parents with strollers. The fragrance from the potted flowers flanked throughout the outdoor space permeated Millicent's olfactory glands and made an inviting impression.

"Who lives here?" The new environment caused Millicent's prying to resurface.

"No one you know," Sammy hissed as he scavenged the area for food.

"Do you know them?"

"Yes!"

"So, who are they?"

"None of your business," Sammy snarled, "Could you be more bothersome?"

It was a rhetorical question, but Millicent felt the need to comment. "If you wanted to be alone, you should've left me under the pergola. You asked me to come here."

"I'm regretting that decision by the second. It's a safe place, leave it at that." Sammy switched his energy from Millicent back to finding food. He dragged a half-devoured croissant from underneath a chair to Millicent, "Maybe this will keep your mouth busy for a while."

Millicent's need to feed took precedence over furthering the argument. She nipped at the flaky, buttery crust while Sammy watched. "Aren't you hungry," she asked.

"Not for food," Sammy replied in his signature creepy tone.

Millicent was hesitant in finishing her next bite. Clarification from Sammy regarding his hunger had to come first. The question; however, never moved past her beak. The presence of a male human centered in the balcony's entrance transformed Millicent and Sammy into statues. The male's body filled the glass door's vertical space. He walked out in loafers and knee length shorts. His gray hair showed his maturity, but it didn't match his defined muscular physique.

With a clear remembrance of her last encounter with humankind, Millicent's first instinct was to run and hide. Since Sammy didn't budge, she didn't either. The man picked up a magazine from the table, then turned to go back inside. Sammy's sudden movement caught his attention.

"American birds eating a croissant, Honey bring me my camera," the man murmured.

Before Honey made an appearance, the man slowly approached Millicent and Sammy. He kneeled down and extended his hand as if he wanted to make peace. Sammy didn't believe his sincerity and made his feelings known.

"Darn it!" The man withdrew his hand. "The little turd bit me."

"What are you going on about out here?" A female's voice carried from inside the home through the door's opening. Before the woman could get a good view of what was going on, Sammy rushed Millicent into the air and to the opposite side of the balcony where they took cover in between two plant stands.

"I got bit by a sparrow that's all."

"A sparrow, where is he?" The lady picked up the croissant. "I'm forbidding you from leaving anymore food out here."

"Don't worry, they're gone and the bleeding's already stopped. I'm fine. It's more funny than serious."

Rapid honking of a car's horn beckoned the couple back inside. "The kids are here," the couple reacted in unison.

Sammy was more interested in seeing the kids than the woman. He took off with Millicent to the front of the house. They landed on top of a row of uniformly cut hedges.

"Look who I found wondering around the airport," the daughter joked before handing the car keys to the now fully clothed male.

The couple greeted their two sons with open arms.

"I'm so glad you decided to spend your summer at home," the mom communicated.

"College is looking good on you boys." The dad gave the boys a once-over.

"Thanks, Dad," the boys responded.

"Let's get you guys situated and catch up before Mom has to go to work. She made a big meal with all your favorites." The father grabbed a handle on one suitcase and the boys held on to the others as everyone walked into the house like the picturesque family.

Sammy flew a safe distance behind the family. He watched them walk away until he couldn't see past the closed door.

"Wow, what a great dad," Sammy said. The source of his sarcasm was hurt.

"But that's a lie because you're their father, aren't you? That's your wife and kids. This is your house. The Romeo, that's your friend. How can they call that betrayer Dad?

Are you alright," Millicent asked. A supportive friend as opposed to a nosey bird might normalize Sammy's attitude. Perhaps the removal of his aggressiveness was a welcomed exchange for the family's comfort and happiness.

Sammy held a long stare at Millicent before he answered, "How ironic, you remember everything about me but nothing about yourself." Sammy's mystique returned. "I changed my mind about staying here. We need to leave."

****

Millicent and Sammy flew the stretch of the city, north, south, east, west, and repeated. It was obvious Sammy was blowing off steam; however, Millicent was exhausted. "Sammy, I can't do this any longer. I need to rest." Millicent found the perfect spot to rejuvenate. She landed in the bottom well of a tiered water feature centered inside a courtyard. The water was not as cool as she'd hoped but it would do. She took a few sips to quench her thirst then submerged her body to douse her flaming limbs. Sammy stood on the edge, admiring his reflection before taking a sip and zoning out.

"You want to talk about it," Millicent volunteered her ears.

"What's there to talk about?"

"How about what it is you're running from?"

Sammy ignored Millicent's question and instead surveyed their surroundings. "Of all the places to land, you would pick here as if my cup wasn't running over with enough sorrow."

"I don't understand." Millicent grew accustomed to using that phrase.

"This is an old folk's home. We're surrounded by bleakness and death." Sammy looked up at an object that stole his concentration.

Millicent's eyes traced Sammy's gaze to a beam of light on the east wing of the senior living facility. They both looked to the west as another beam shined on the opposite end.

"You don't want to miss this." Sammy forced Millicent up in the air. They landed on the top of the building's eastside, hopped closer to the light and waited. It didn't take long before an old, weary man floated through the worn shingles of the building.

"Let's get a look at contestant number two."

Sammy hurried Millicent to the second light where they watched an elderly woman drift up in the direction of the unknown. Next, he led her to the clock tower positioned on top of the center section of the building.

"Now we wait," Sammy directed as he watched both images elevate.

"Wait for what?"

"To see which one makes the idiotic mistake of thinking they can change their fate like we did." Sammy faced Millicent. "You want to know what I'm running from, it's that." Sammy looked back at the lights. "My arrogance, my ignorance, it's every selfish emotion that landed me here instead of up there. Seeing my creations call that traitor Dad, you have no idea how that makes me feel. So, I fly to forget, or I sit and hope for company."

Sammy and Millicent's heads flip flopped from left to right as they watched both beams of light hoist their target higher and higher.

"Let's go back to the pergola. I'll apologize to Anna. I'm sure she'll forgive me and let us stay there."

"Are you scared," Sammy inquired.

Yes! "No, but I don't think this is the ideal place for either of us to be emotionally. Let's go back to Anna's unless you have a better location."

"As a matter of fact, I do." Sammy leaped into the air, headed toward one of the beams. He circled the light and the passenger for a way in, and out of his chosen misery. He tailed them all the way to the base of a cloud. Sammy was past his acceptance date, denied access and left solo in the sky.

Millicent suspected this wasn't his first attempt. She didn't know what would comfort Sammy's rejection. "Sammy...."

"Don't say a word Small, just follow me."

Millicent obeyed.

****

The sun set on a whirlwind day and all Millicent remembered was ticking off the one sparrow who wanted to help her and making friends with an unstable instigator. She and Sammy trekked a lengthy distance before he announced their flight destination. "Small, do you see that big tree?" Millicent's eyes followed Sammy's wing pointing to an oak shading a convenience store. "That's where we're going," he briefed. They descended and escaped into the thick foliage of the mammoth tree. "This branch will do." Sammy landed with Millicent plopping down beside him. Her flying improved but her landing still needed practice.

"Why so far out?"

"It's not far out. The shopping center is right up the road. Don't you remember...." Sammy slowed the pace of his tongue and allowed his brain a chance to catch up. "Of course you don't remember, you've blown a fuse in your thinker. This is the heart of the city, prime real estate, party central, where all the fun happens."

"Party central?" Millicent had an overly exciting day. She loathed the inkling of a party. "I'm not trying to party.

The one thing I want to do is get my memory back."

"Loosen up and relive a little, Small. Let me show you how to make the best of this sparrow situation so you can stop being a wet blanket. Also, please don't embarrass me in front of our guests."

"What guests?"

Sammy moved Millicent to a clearing in the tree's leaves. They peered out at the sky. It glowed with wispy variations of copper and rose hues as if they tiptoed off an artist's brush. A mobile black mass obstructed their artwork. As the thick mass closed in, Millicent discovered it was hundreds of sparrows. They darted through the leaves, all in harmony until each found a suitable branch to relax. Upon their arrival, mindless chatter and music saturated the night air. Even the crows showed up. Some soared above while others scampered below. Millicent was unsure if they were joining, crashing or observing the festivities.

"Sammy, where's the music coming from?"

"There's a club up the street with a rooftop dance floor." The party animal smoldered in Sammy. "They play Hip-Hop, R&B and Soul music from seven p.m. to midnight."

"No way am I staying here," Millicent protested.

"Fine, go back to Anna and the boring suburbs."

"I would, but I don't know the way. You're going to have to take me back."

"Of course, after midnight" Sammy discontinued his discussion with Millicent and engrossed himself with his guests.

Lonesomeness was the one memory Millicent wished to abolish. She zipped from the tree to a nearby dumpster on the hunt for something to eat and figure out her next move. She hit the jackpot. Old donuts, chicken and hot dogs beat stale bread any day. Her parched throat craved something to cleanse her palate.

"Hey Sammy, he's got beer," a partygoer from the tree boasted as a couple walked from the convenience store to the parking lot.

The female held a small bag and her male companion had a case of beer. Sammy locked in on the alcohol then charged. He streaked out of the tree, leaving branches bare, dived down on the unsuspecting male, pecked at his head and tried to get him to drop the goods. Sammy struggled to complete the task, other sparrows joined in. To evade the attack, the couple dropped their packages and raised their arms in the fashion of a car dealership's wind machine character. They retreated to their car and drove off. Meanwhile, their attackers towed the beer away. It spewed slightly from impact and left a trail that led back to their hideout. A cleanup crew of crows sipped up all the liquor so the actions could not be pinned to the habitants of the tree. It also erased the likelihood that any beer-loving rodents would be tempted to steal what they stole. The only thing on the ground was a small brown bag with egg yolk running out of the bottom. Millicent watched the runny mess and smiled about an unlocked joke in her head.

"Runny eggs…at breakfast…they were all laughing. They said my eggs were runny. I remember something from my human life!" Millicent left the dumpster and flew behind the tree where Sammy and the other birds used their beaks to puncture the beer cans and enjoyed the spoils of their victory. "Sammy, I remember they said my eggs where runny at breakfast. They were joking about my eggs. Sammy, did you hear what I said? I remember something!"

"Good for you," Sammy stammered, "now leave so I can get drunk and forget."

Somehow, Millicent wasn't bewildered at the statement spoken by her intoxicated friend. Her head hung low as she returned to the dumpster to recollect more. She closed her eyes and concentrated. She saw herself sitting at a table looking down at a plate. A masculine voice was reciting a prayer. There was laughter from girls. Millicent dredged up the memories of her husband and kids. A more gruesome appearance of a pool of blood with a head floating in it entered her mind.

"Oh no, did I kill my family for making fun of my eggs? Am I a psycho? It makes sense." Millicent strolled the edge of the dumpster like a courtroom lawyer during cross-examination. "I was rushing to avoid capture and I had an accident." She switched from prosecution to defense as an accurate account surfaced. "Wait, wait, it was a doll's head in the washer. I was doing laundry. This is good, what else. Think Millicent, think. Millicent, my name is Millicent!"

Millicent raced back to Sammy with hopes her new information was big enough to garner a better reaction. Optimism left when she discovered him alone, on a branch, lashing out at the world in a drunken stupor. He cursed God, his wife and kids, whom he said he loved. The others joined in to air out their grievances in the night. Echoing cries of desolation interpreted by any human passersby as sweet lullabies from birds were, in reality, the voices of tormented souls. Millicent figured out Sammy's intention. His misery wanted her company. The tree wasn't a healthy environment either. Millicent shouldn't be there.

I'M SORRY

The glow from Penny's bedroom was on the high end of the color spectrum compared to the evening light outside. Inside the room, the child searched for a conversation piece. Her bird buddies knew the names of all her stuffed animals, dolls and favorite games. Tonight she had a serious topic to discuss.

"Here's the new picture of my family. It's the best one because my eyes aren't closed and my sister's not sticking out her tongue." Penny kneeled on top of her desk and held a silver plated frame in front of her opened bedroom window. With her desk lamp as a lighted backdrop, Penny pointed to each member of her family. "This is me right here, my daddy, my big sis and my mommy. I'm going to draw a picture to take to Mommy to make her feel better. She's in the hospital. She was in a very bad car crash this morning. She's sleeping now, but she's going to wake up. She's not going to die," in a low, teary voice Penny added, "not like my sissy's mom and little brother." The possibility of her mother dying was too much for the child to process.

"Penny, who are you talking to?" Valerie and Brian burst into Penny's room expecting an intruder.

Upon their entry, Penny jumped from the top of her desk, to her chair, to the floor with the family portrait in tow like a seasoned acrobat. She didn't want her day to end with a scolding for standing on the furniture. The two sparrows she was chatting with flew away.

"Was that a bird," Brian quizzed.

"Yes Daddy, I was telling them about Mommy," Penny innocently replied.

"She talks to birds," Valerie whispered to Brian.

"It's nothing, Ma," Brian insisted but began to suspect otherwise.

"Sweetheart, I want to talk to you about everything that's happening today. Come sit by Nana." Valerie motioned for Penny to join her on the bed while Brian took a seat on a pink, fuzzy beanbag chair.

Penny let the smiling faces inside the frame watch the sky mature into nightfall while she joined Valerie.

"Today's been a tough day for you hasn't it, Honey?" Valerie ran her hand down the length of one of Penny's plaits. Cognizant of what resulted from that move, Penny pushed Valerie's hand away. "Penny, I apologize for the bad things I said about your mother. I was wrong. Do you forgive me? Can we be friends again?" Valerie's French tipped nails tickled Penny's thigh as she awaited her response.

"No!" Penny swatted Valerie's hands for release and stomped to her preferred spot at her bookshelf to play with her displayed dolls.

Valerie was peeved that Penny would be this disrespectful. "No?"

Penny's attention rested on her dolls as she explained her response, "You don't mean it. There was a boy in my class named Bobby Green and he would pull my hair. I told the teacher and the teacher asked him to stop and made him say he was sorry. He said he was sorry, but he pulled my hair again when the teacher wasn't looking. I asked Mommy why he did it again if he said he was sorry. She said that the only reason he said he was sorry was because Mrs. Swanson made him say it, and he really wasn't sorry. Daddy made you say you're sorry. You don't mean it, and you'll just hurt my feelings again. Mommy also said that she could tell when a person means something or not because she can look deep into their eyes and tell if what they are saying is coming from their heart. Mommy said I don't have those powers yet, but I'll get them when I get older. If I can't do it," Penny turned to Valerie and gave her an ultimatum, "when Mommy is better you can say you're sorry to her and if she believes you, I'll believe you."

"Fine, we will revisit this once Millicent is well." Valerie wasted no time exiting Penny's room with Brian a half pace behind her.

"Mom, she's right," Brian gave validity to Penny's speculation.

"Remember when I said your wife was turning my grandchildren against me?" Valerie blamed her misfortunes as a grandmother on Millicent.

"Ma, that had nothing to do with your conspiracy theory about Millicent. It was about some boy in her class. Face it, Penny figured out you weren't sincere. I don't know what it's going to take to fix the relationship between you and Millicent if the fact that she's laying in a coma right now doesn't trigger your sense of compassion. Maybe knowing that the tie between you and your youngest granddaughter depends on it will unfreeze your heart." Brian brushed past Valerie down the stairs. He narrowly avoided a collision with Brianna as she made her way up.

Brianna entered Penny's room and fastened the door behind her. "Hey, what was that all about?"

Penny sat at her desk and worked on a new drawing to take to her mother. "What was what all about?"

"What happened with you, Nana and Dad? They looked upset. What did you say to them?"

"I told the truth."

"I guess the truth does hurt. What are you drawing?" Brianna picked Penny up, took over her chair, and placed Penny in her lap.

"It's a picture for Mommy."

"It looks pretty. Are those birds?" Brianna tapped the two gray blobs with wings at the top of the page.

"Yeah, the ones that come to my window and I talk to. Don't laugh and say that I'm cuckoo like you did before."

"Hey, it's my right as a big sister to make fun of you and get under your skin." Brianna poked Penny's belly. "I still love you, and Nana loves you too."

Penny rolled her eyes at the mention of Valerie's name. "She doesn't love Mommy, and I came from Mommy. So if she doesn't love her, I don't see how she can love me."

Realizing that her little sister was far more intelligent than any ordinary child, Brianna tried to explain, "See Penny, adults can be very complicated. I don't think Nana hates Millicent, she just blames her for the unresolved issues in this family."

"You blame her too. You said you wished she was dead. You're just like Nana. You don't like me or Mommy either." Penny gave Brianna the same cold shoulder reserved for Valerie and laid down on her bed.

"But, I took it back," Brianna proclaimed. Unwilling to bear Penny likening their grandmother to her, Brianna dragged the desk chair to the bed to finish her explanation, "I was angry when I said that because, at the time, I did blame Millicent, but it wasn't her fault. Your mom just wanted us to be one happy family."

"What's wrong with that?" Penny sat up in her bed ready to hear the answer from her sister.

Brianna meditated on Penny's question and had an epiphany. She mirrored Millicent. What the two of them fought so hard for wasn't dominance but acceptance, baggage and all. "There's nothing wrong with it, but I'm half of another family that shouldn't be forgotten about either. Do you kind of get what I'm saying?"

"Yeah, we should be two happy families," Penny concluded.

"That's right," Brianna congratulated her sister's wisdom.

"How can we get everyone to be happy?"

"I think counseling would work, but Nana's stubborn. It's going to take her and Millicent, I mean Mom, when she gets better, sitting down together, just the two of them, and talking things out so they can better understand each other. That way they don't keep hurting each other which eventually ends up hurting us." Calling Millicent mom still didn't feel right to Brianna, but she was doing all she could to appeal to Penny.

"Yeah, grownups are going to have to start acting like grownups?"

"Exactly Penny, then there will be no more fighting, and everyone will get along. We're going to love and respect one another and be one big, happy, blended family."

"You promise?"

"I promise." Brianna crossed her heart with her fingers, to show Penny she was sincere and gave her little sister a hug.

The two siblings shared a rare moment and enjoyed the fact that they overtook the positions as the mature ones of the household. Back at her desk, Penny sat in her sister's lap and they both worked to finish the drawing. They postponed their project when one of the sparrows that hid from Brian and Valerie earlier revisited Penny's window. It first landed on the window ledge. Next, with no hesitation, it made itself welcomed inside the room.

"Don't be afraid," Penny shared with Brianna, "it's not going to hurt you. It's a nice bird."

"I'm not afraid." Brianna's words indicated her bravery; however, her clinched teeth and robotic speech signified otherwise. "What is it doing?"

The bird's fascination with Brianna was undeniable as it

inched closer to her. Locked in a deep gaze, the bird stopped moving and spoke, "My precious baby girl, I'm so happy to see you. It's been a long time. I know you're not going to believe this, but it's me." The bird advanced toward Brianna with its wings spread wide open as if it expected a warm embrace. "I never left you. I've been here watching over you. I love you always."

Penny and Brianna only heard chirps from the small creature that they tried to imitate. The duo laughed at the bird and their odd conduct.

"Girls, get down here! We need to get back to the hospital before it gets too late." Brian's voice drifted through the room like a cold draft.

"Penny, we better go."

Penny grabbed her picture and markers so she could finish her artwork in the car while Brianna fanned the bird out of the window. "Shoo, we don't have time to play anymore we need to go and be with our mother." She closed and locked the window before she followed Penny out of the room.

"Why do you continue to do this, Anna," Gladys sought an answer as she reappeared at the window from her hiding place.

"When did Brianna start calling Millicent mom?" Brianna's use of that word was worse than death to Anna. "She needs to see me Gladys, not this beak and feathers form of me. She needs to see the flesh and blood Marianna Hamilton. I'm her mother. She needs to hear me say I love her. We were in a rush to get to the hospital that day I didn't tell her. She needs to hear it come from my mouth one last time, maybe then I can move on." Anna couldn't convince herself. "What am I saying, I can't leave my baby here to be an outsider in her own home. Why does she have to suffer? Haven't I suffered enough for her too?" Anna directed her questions to the heavens and waited for an answer. Gladys was the lone voice she heard.

"Anna, she's not suffering."

"Are you watching the same child? Ever since she turned thirteen, Brianna has been on a downward spiral. She's hanging out with misfits, skipping class, sneaking out, having boys climb into her bedroom. If I hadn't placed that bee's nest on the trellis who knows what type of trouble she'd be in. Brian's inept to handle her. Look at the way he handled me. He'd probably try to lock her up in her room until she turned thirty. Being a mama's boy doesn't give you motherly instincts."

"But Millicent's there and she cares about Brianna," said Gladys.

"Millicent's only pretending. She doesn't want to be a mother or a wife. Millicent wants the titles. She treats Brian and the girls like her clients, always bargaining, negotiating and caving in to their demands. She thinks she's trying to close a deal, not run a household. Plus, she plays favorites. You know that Brianna needs her real mother." Anna eyeballed Gladys for agreement, she didn't gain it but powered on. "Actually, they all need me. I'm the one who wants to be there for them."

"You know that will never happen."

"Never, you still believe in that word, Gladys. You were so determined to right your wrong of giving me up for adoption that you found me beyond the grave. So, 'never' is not going to stop me from trying either."

****

Millicent missed her window to venture out on her own. Night covered everything like a quilt. She waited by the dumpster and put her faith in Sammy to keep his promise. To run down the clock, Millicent concentrated on more of her past but the loud music and squawking drove away any loosely formed thoughts.

"Shut up," Millicent shouted.

Someone heard and granted her wish for quiet, temporarily. Within minutes, the music from the club cranked up again; this time with a more mellow sound like a love ballad. The sparrows fled the tree in pairs. They swirled in sync with the music as they performed for the eye in the sky. Millicent felt like the unattractive new girl who lurked on the sidelines while the other sparrows formed circles, inside of circles, inside of circles. The formation resembled the ripples in the puddle of soured milk smelling dumpster juices Millicent waded in.

****

Back at Calverton Memorial, the Hamilton family headed to Millicent's room with their goodies from home.

"Excuse me." Penny's preoccupation with her masterpiece caused her to bump into a doctor conversing at the nurse's station. The impact sent her staggering backwards and her drawing to the floor.

"No worries, Princess." The doctor picked up the piece of paper and studied the artwork.

"Do you like it?" Penny offered her lovely smile in hopes she received an equally loving compliment.

The doctor analyzed the vine-covered pergola attached to a white house with two birds flying above and a child observing it all from her front row seat in the window. "It's beautiful. Did you draw this?"

"Yes. It's for my mom. She's in a long sleep like the lady from the cartoon. This is our house here, our patio and these are the birds that I talk to from my window."

Brian watched the doctor's eyes trace every line on the piece of paper. He convinced himself she was on the verge of a diagnosis for his daughter without his consent. He intervened, "Hello doctor, my name is Brian Hamilton. This is my very imaginative daughter Penny, my daughter Bri and my mother Valerie. My wife, Millicent, was in an awful accident and is in a coma. We decided to bring some of her things from home to liven up the room."

The doctor was mesmerized by the picture but forced herself to look away in order to make her introduction, "Hi, I'm Dr. Miller. Sorry to hear that about your wife, I know how difficult this must be on you and your family. Luckily, I can be of service. I'm a family therapist."

Brianna's face gleamed. This chance meeting had to be a divine encounter.

"No, that's not necessary. I'm sure talking to birds is a phase. Besides, she was doing that way before the accident." Brian returned the picture to Penny and rustled his family back on the path to Millicent's room.

"I'm sure it is." Dr. Miller grabbed Brian by the forearm, preventing his retreat. "But I specialize in helping families where one member is in long term care like a coma," Dr. Miller's voice softened as she concluded, "or other extreme cases."

"I think that's a great idea," Brianna shifted the box of home decor from one hip to the other and accepted the offer before her dad could give a polite rejection, "This family could use a sit-down session with a professional, the sooner the better." Brianna looked at her father. "We've been quiet for too long."

"Fantastic, well let me check my schedule. I can give you a call to set up a meeting as soon as possible."

Brian gave in. "That will be fine, Dr. Miller." He reached in his pocket and retrieved his wallet. "Here's my business card. You can reach me on my cell."

Dr. Miller accepted the card. "Hamilton Construction, so you finally fulfilled your dream and started your own company. I love it! Good for you."

"Pardon me," Brian asked. The doctor's interest in his business puzzled him.

Dr. Miller tried to regain her professionalism. "The establishment year on your card, that's this year. I have a couple of friends who are becoming entrepreneurs. I'm proud more people are living their dreams."

"Oh, thanks!" The doctor's gracious, enthusiasm was foreign to Brian who accompanied his reply with a prepubescent smile.

Unimpressed with her dad's distraction from family business, Brianna butted in, "Dad, this stuff is getting heavy. Can we go and decorate the room now?"

"Of course, let's go decorate ladies."

****

The family went into Millicent's room and saw Pamela standing at the foot of the hospital bed sobbing. Brian's embrace was ineffective. Pamela buried her head in his chest. She confessed through her hidden tears, "It's my fault. It was my responsibility to get the samples. Keisha wasn't sick. I lied because I forgot. This is all my fault."

"It's OK, Pamela." Valerie tried to console her; however, it made Pamela more hysterical.

"I'm the reason she's here. It's my fault," Pamela continued to insist.

Brian clamped Pamela by her arms. He reprimanded her like one of his children. "Calm down Pamela! It was an accident. It's not your fault, so stop crying before you upset the girls."

Pamela submitted to Brian for the sake of the kids. "Hey girls, Bri, Pinwheel, are you two good?"

Brianna responded first, "Yeah, Auntie."

"Yes," Penny remarked, "I'm OK. Don't worry Auntie Pamela, Mommy is going to get better."

Pamela concurred, "You're right, she is."

With the drama subsided, the family arranged the container full of mementos they gathered from home amongst the bouquets of flowers, balloons and cards delivered from Millicent's co-workers, clients and associates.

"Daddy, don't forget my picture." Penny handed her drawing to Brian who pinned it in the middle of a bare corkboard that hung on the wall opposite the windows.

"Have you spoken to her physician, Brian? What did they say," Pamela asked.

"They're doing the best they can. They don't know when she will regain consciousness though."

"Daddy," Penny requested her father's attention, "my tummy hurts."

"That's right, we never did eat breakfast. You girls haven't eaten anything all day. You must be starving."

"They have a decent cafeteria here," Pamela noted. "Girls let's go get something to eat. Do you want to come with us Mrs. Valerie?"

"No thank you Pamela, I'll stay here." Valerie rested in a seat across from Millicent's bed.

"Are you sure, Mom," Brian asked.

"Yes, you go eat. I'll be fine here."

"I'll bring you something back anyway, Ma."

Brian, Pamela and the girls exited the room leaving Valerie behind to watch over Millicent.

Valerie sat and waited with crossed limbs and a frown. Her nosiness made it impossible for her to remain sitting too long. She walked around the room, smelled the floral arrangements and read the attached cards. Her eyes rolled at the amount of attention received from a car accident.

"Aren't you the prosperous businesswoman? Get better soon from Bob Montgomery, prayers to you and your family from Cecil Lete. I should have known all male acquaintances. Look at this big, beautiful bouquet of red roses. I wonder who sent them." Valerie opened the affixed envelope with her index finger and retrieved the card from inside. "What type of greeting is Pretty Lady from a client?" Valerie read the letter aloud in a male admirer's voice.

> *I'm on my knees praying for you right now. You mean the world to me and there's no way I'm letting you leave this earth. You're one of the strongest women I know so I'm sure you'll pull through.*

"I love you!" Valerie returned to her normal diction. "Wait until Brian sees this."

****

Millicent reveled in what the droplets signified. Rain would ruin their party. She stretched out her wing in anticipation for another drop, nothing happened. The ripples at her feet were still now as well. She looked up to read the clouds only to find a large cat prowling overhead on the dumpster's lid with an opened, saliva drenched mouth ready to pounce. Before she could become the feline's late-night snack, Sammy feverishly clawed at the cat's body. He pecked into its skin until blood trickled onto the cat's fur. Unfazed by the cat's wimpy meows for mercy, Sammy continued his torture. Millicent feared he was going to kill it.

"Sammy, that's enough," Millicent hollered.

The mangled cat leaped for its life off the dumpster and staggered away.

"Small, this is the second time I saved your life today. I should get a big reward."

"Not when it's always your fault I'm put in danger."

"I'm going to pretend you said thank you Sammy. Why are you hanging around dumpsters anyway? You're just asking for it, Small."

"My name is Millicent Hamilton. My memory's coming back."

"Oh, well Millicent do you want to join me in a dance with the others?"

Millicent played down her excitement. "I guess." She was grateful for Sammy's heroic act and the invitation.

"Great! When you hear one and two, girls fly up to the stars. When you hear three and four girls, fly east. Got it?"

Millicent reiterated the instructions to Sammy's liking as they dashed off together to join the rest of the birds.

All Millicent lacked was a flowing gown to enhance the dramatics of her aerial twirls. Sammy led her with charisma she didn't realize he possessed. He caressed her feathers while they glided into spherical formations. She pondered if she ever felt this liberated.

A husky voice gave the command and the dance partners parted ways as the women took off toward the stars. Next, the voice screamed, "Return," and the females circled down to meet up with the men. The two sexes stayed together for a while until the command, "Three and four," filled the air. Millicent knew she needed to go east but she didn't know east from west. She took a guess and followed the crowd. She figured out her choice was wrong when she and Sammy met up again.

"Millicent, this isn't east, but you can stay with me since it's your first time."

Sammy and Millicent continued to mesmerize the moon with their seductive, patterned dance for several hours until the music stopped. The bold colored strung lights on the club's rooftop went shy and the patrons exited the building. The florescent bulbs at the convenience store blinked off before its gated fortress closed for business. The party was over. The sparrows retreated in pairs of two, male and female, to the tree. Sammy and Millicent were alone in the sky. They looked at each other, smiled and continued to dance to a rhythm of their own composed from memories Millicent had yet to regain and Sammy had long since suppressed. Millicent felt so alive and at peace. She no longer cared if this was her normal disposition. She was never forgetting this moment. They danced until tiredness got the best of them.

"Do you want to go to the tree with me Millicent," Sammy propositioned.

****

Brian returned to the room holding two sandwiches and two bags of chips in one hand. The other hand firmly gripped two bottled sodas. "See what, Ma?"

Valerie approached her son with I told you so excitement. "Look." She handed the card to Brian. "I knew something adulterous was happening with your wife and her clients. Read it. I knew she was trying to pull the wool over your eyes. She had you fooled Son, but I knew she's been playing you all this time. She's a tramp," Valerie whispered her last sentence but her point was loud and clear.

Brian struggled to juggle the note and the snacks in his hand, he skimmed over the card then asked his mother, "How much did you read?"

"To where this loser said he loves the woman you're married to. That's far enough don't you think?"

"Read the rest of the note out loud." Brian handed the card back to Valerie and she obliged.

You're the bright spot of my day. It makes me and my wife proud to see women like you make a name for yourself in this He-Man world and do it with such class. Brian is a very lucky man. Hey Brian, don't hesitate to call the Mrs. and me if you need anything.
God Bless,
Tom and Larna Barnes
P.S. - Your accident made front page. I'll hold a copy for you to pick up when you come back.

Valerie, with shame smudged on her face, attached the card back onto the bouquet and turned to Brian.

Once again disappointed with his mother, Brian explained, "Tom owns the newsstand in her office building. A while back, Millicent fought for him when management wanted to close it down. They've been friends ever since. We've been going to church with him and his wife for a couple of months now. What's it going to take for you to get it? I'm going back down to eat with the girls and Pamela." Brian handed Valerie her share of the food and walked out of the room.

Embarrassed, Valerie slumped down in a chair. An invisible line drawn down the tiled floor pitted her against Millicent. The more dirt she tried to uncover the more Millicent came away squeaky-clean. Proving Millicent's innocence was never Valerie's intention.

****

Millicent felt the anticipation in Sammy's voice as he waited for her answer. His eyes, on the contrary, showed he was prepared to be let down. Even though she enjoyed this side of Sammy, Millicent couldn't forget his devious personality.

"I believe we should go back to the pergola."

"This can be your home. I'll protect you. I've been doing that all day, haven't I? I'll keep protecting you. You'll be safe. Look, we don't have to go to the tree. We can go on the roof and I can help you remember more from your past. What do you Sarah…I mean say, Milli?"

With that plea, Millicent uncovered other flashbacks of her husband. Their disputes were frequent lately. Brian called her Milli once temperatures cooled down and he wanted to get back in her good grace, similar to Sammy's attempt. Aside from their arguments, Brian loved her and she him. Although appreciative of Sammy's affection, nothing would make Millicent stay with him. Even though she was a bird, she'd never betray Brian.

Millicent answered, "I think it would be better if you took me back to Anna's house."

"Anna! Anna! Anna! You're an idiot to be following her and you don't even know it!" Sammy's abrasiveness reappeared.

Whether it was for her rejection, befriending him, or her attitude, Millicent felt the need to apologize, "Sammy, I'm sorry."

That word conjured a sleeping monster. "Don't feel sorry for me!" Sammy lunged at Millicent and embedded his claws in her wings. She tried to defend herself but anger multiplied his strength as he shook her like a rag doll." After all I've done for you, you leave me here alone. You never loved me. You never cared about me. You should be here. You should be here with me." He tore into

Millicent until feathers dropped and blood gushed. The cat was fortunate. "Don't ever feel sorry for me Sarah!"

"Sammy stop, you're hurting me! I'm not Sarah! I'm Millicent," Millicent corrected while pleading for her life.

Hearing Millicent's name tamed the beast and Sammy returned to his level of normal but with no apology for his actions. "Don't you ever feel sorry for me, you got that! Now, let's get you back to Anna."

Although Millicent's entire body trembled from horror and pain, she followed Sammy anyway. On their way to Anna's house, he yelled out flight directions and made notes of landmarks to ensure Millicent could find her way back to him and the tree. He was dead wrong if he expected her to return.

****

Valerie opened her bag of chips and nestled it between her legs. She set her soda on the floor, pulled the plastic wrapping from around the sandwich and took a ravenous bite. As she sat and ate in a dull corner of the room staring at her daughter-in-law surrounded by love and vibrancy, something started to click. Valerie's face showed the expression of a light bulb coming on at last. She stood up, tossing the remaining bites of food in her abandoned seat and crossed the line.

"You win. You're better than me. You're better than Mari. You must be the first woman in history to master the balance between career, motherhood and marriage." Valerie's cynicism made a brief appearance in her revelation. "You win! I've been so angry with you because I'm not you. I gave up my dreams when I got married and had Brian because that's what everyone told me to do. I saw every woman in my life devote their lives to their husband and kids. I wanted to pass this on to every woman who came into my son's life, but you wouldn't hear of it. You were smart not to listen. You always made me wonder what if I hadn't listened. I would censor those ideas by telling myself at least I was a better mother, but that was a lie. Forcing upon someone else what others forced fed me makes me as guilty as the original enforcer. You broke the cycle and you are the better wife, mother and professional because you never let anyone limit you. You've always been a free bird and I'm sorry I've been such a pain in the ass to you. I promise to do better." Valerie sealed the deal with a handshake. While holding her hand, Valerie felt Millicent's grip tighten. "Oh my God, nurse! Nurse, get in here now!"

Two nurses entered the room with Brian, Pamela and the girls on their heels. The family heard Valerie's frantic call for assistance as they got off the elevator.

Brian spoke first, "Mom, what did you do?"

"Nothing, Millicent squeezed my hand. Look!" Valerie pointed down to the firm grip of a person fighting for their life.

A nurse replaced Valerie's hand and examined Millicent's condition.

"Ma, what were you doing?"

"I was holding her hand and apologizing for being such a pain in the butt. I felt her squeeze back. I promise I'm not making this up. She squeezed back. You all saw it, right?"

"Does this mean she's waking up," Brianna asked.

"No, it's Mommy saying she forgives you," Penny diagnosed. "You're telling the truth, you're really sorry. Mommy forgives you and since she forgives you, I forgive you too." Penny suffocated her grandmother's waist with her body. Valerie held her youngest grandchild into her arms, ecstatic at their reconciliation.

"Nurse, is she waking up," Brianna asked again.

The two nurses looked at each other and in agreement,

the head nurse concluded, "She's not responding now."

"But moving is a good sign isn't it," Pamela asked. "It means she's getting better doesn't it?"

The nurse didn't want to give the family unfounded information. "I think it's best everyone keeps an optimistic attitude. We will continue to monitor her condition. Hopefully, her hand movement will be a promising sign."

"I hate to interrupt," the second nurse chimed in, "but it's our policy to limit overnight guest to one person. Mr. Hamilton, you can stay if you wish, but I'll have to ask the rest of you to return after ten a.m." With that, the two nurses departed.

"I can take Mrs. Valerie and the kids home if you want to stay Brian," Pamela suggested.

"Thanks, Pamela," Brian said.

After everyone said their goodbyes and Pamela, Valerie and the girls left, Brian gathered two chairs to form a makeshift bed near Millicent's left side. He laid with his head near her feet so his face would be the first thing she saw when she opened her eyes. He took her hand in his and settled in for the night.

****

Before they could make it to Pamela's car, Penny had an urgent matter that needed attention. "I have to go to the bathroom."

"Pinwheel, can you hold it until you get home?"

"No Auntie, I need to go now."

"Don't worry, I'll take her." Brianna grabbed Penny's hand and they walked back into the hospital.

"Make it quick girls," Valerie instructed. "Pamela and I will be parked out front."

"We will," Penny and Brianna responded.

The sisters walked towards the lobby restrooms but a

closed for cleaning sign stopped them from entering.

"Penny, let's just go back to Mom's room," Brianna instructed. "Dad's probably sleeping, so we need to be very quiet so we don't wake him."

"Got it," Penny whispered back to her sister.

The door to Millicent's room was open. The pair walked in. Brianna showed Penny to the restroom on the side of the short entryway and closed the door to give the child her privacy. Brianna continued into the room to check on her parents. Her father's loud snoring muffled her footsteps. She was surprised to see Dr. Miller hovering over them.

Whispering, "Dr. Miller, what are you doing in here?"

Startled, Dr. Miller replied in a whisper. "Brianna, I was…" Dr. Miller's head surveyed the room to come up with an adequate excuse. "I saw the light on and I came in to speak with your father about my services. When I saw him asleep, I was going to turn off the lights and leave."

"It doesn't take long to flip a light switch. Why were you standing over them, watching them sleep? Are you some type of freak?"

By this time, Penny was finished in the restroom. "You're the doctor who liked my picture. What are you doing here? Did you want to see it again?"

Dr. Miller attempted to give Penny the same story she told Brianna, "No—"

Brianna interrupted the doctor's explanation, "No, she was leaving. Right, Doc?"

"Right, I was leaving."

The trio, with Penny as lead and Brianna in the rear, walked to the door.

"Aren't you forgetting what you came to do, Dr. Miller?"

"Oh yes." The doctor turned off the lights as she made her way out the room. "I will stop by in the morning to speak with your father."

Brianna gently pulled the door closed but she wasn't finished with Dr. Miller. "I don't think we will need your services after all."

"Brianna, sweetheart, I can help you in more ways than you can even imagine."

"You just want my dad and I don't need your help! I want you to hear me clearly, Dr. Miller." Brianna squared up to the therapist. "You stay away from my father and my family. Consider this your first and final warning. Come on Penny!"

The doctor and Penny watched Brianna head down the hall.

"She's so mean. You should tell Daddy she needs a spanking."

"No, she's being protective. Penny, promise me you'll keep your wild imagination."

Penny wasn't sure what Dr. Miller meant. Since she was able to keep something, she agreed, "I will."

"Have a good night, Penny."

"Good night. I still think you should tell Daddy to spank her." Penny skipped away to catch up with her sister.

CAN'T SAY GOODBYE

Sammy and Millicent arrived back to the pergola. "You're welcome," were Sammy's parting words to Millicent. She wasn't interested in Sammy's goodbye and was thankful to see him fly away. She searched for Anna and Gladys ready to tell them her name and all that she remembered. Millicent hoped her rudeness from earlier was forgiven.

"Where are they?" Millicent circled the perimeter before she spotted Anna and Gladys on the ledge of an upstairs window. She landed in the recess of a dormer with a changed attitude. Afraid of the reaction her presence might bring, she tried to come up with a good opening liner.

"Anna, Gladys. I first want to say I'm—"

"What in the world happened to you?" Anna eyes asked the question before the words left her mouth. "Who did this to you?"

"What are you talking about?"

Without answering Millicent's question, Anna held her by one wing and Gladys grab the other. They led her inside the room to a dresser topped with a mirror covered in a layer of dust. Anna used her wing to remove some of the dust. Millicent looked at her reflection and gasped.

"Oh my God," erupted out of Millicent's mouth. The pain was numb, but her appearance was horrific.

"You went off with Sammy, didn't you," Anna asked, "He did this?"

"Yeah, he turned crazy and attacked me."

"He was always crazy. That's why I warned you about him. You didn't listen."

Here we go with the chastising again. "Don't blame me.

I'm the victim here."

"It's always about you, isn't it?" Anna wasn't letting up.

"Yes! Especially when I'm the only one bleeding with feathers missing."

"Did you do anything to upset him," Gladys asked.

"She didn't have to do anything, remember what happened to Sarah? He's a nut and I tried to warn her."

"OK, I get it. You tried to warn me, I didn't listen, let's move on already." Millicent assessed her wounds and determined she'd live to fight another day. "I came back to apologize to you and your mother, but I'm suddenly not feeling regretful for thinking you're a bully."

"Did you say my mother?" Anna bypassed Millicent calling her a bully for a second time and honed in on another part of her apology. "How did you know Gladys is my mother?"

"Sammy told me."

"Sarah's the only sparrow I told about you," Anna told Gladys. She turned her attention back to Millicent as she explained, "I wanted the others to heed my advice so they would be spared the misery I suffer everyday of this bird life. I didn't want them to miss the message since I have a loved one on this side to comfort me. What else did Sammy tell you? Did he say anything about where Sarah is?"

"No, but he did call me her when he was plucking the stuffing out of me. You've mentioned Sarah to me before too. Who is she?"

Gladys joined in, "She's his wife. Anna found them together and brought them here. Sarah was pleasant. She was a Small, like you. Sammy was very arrogant and troubled."

"He attacked her too," Anna picked up where Gladys left off. "How such an accomplished woman could end up with an abusive psychopath is beyond me. Poor thing couldn't escape his abuse even in death. It's his fault she was even here. She remembered and told me in secrecy that it was a murder-suicide. Sarah said Sammy had a bipolar condition. They diagnosed him in the military before his dishonorable discharge. One minute he was a prince the next he would be accusing her of infidelity. Death also fascinated him and equaled a combination for disaster. On the night of their passing, they were coming home from a nightclub when they got into an explosive argument. Maybe it was the alcohol, or Sammy being Sammy, when he drove their car off the road. He crashed it into a huge oak tree. They were dead on impact. Out of fright, Sarah followed him away from the light. A couple of months after I brought them here, they both disappeared. I guess he felt threatened by our friendship. Sarah had someone else to listen to who had her best interests at heart. After some years passed, I would see Sammy around town without Sarah. I always hoped she was finally able to leave him and find happiness somewhere else. I was surprised to hear Sammy's name since it's been so long. More surprised he would be brave enough to come back here knowing how much I despise him."

Millicent had difficulty piecing Anna's facts with Sammy's facts. "Wait, he told me he died of a heart attack and his wife remarried his friend. He would go back to his old home and watch over his family until he couldn't take seeing them move on without him."

"Believing in lying psychopaths is how you end up with missing feathers," Anna said in her customary, righteous tone. "I wish we knew what happened to Sarah."

"Maybe he lied about how his death happened but not Sarah. I saw her, in human form, with the golf buddy, replacement father and his three kids."

"Did you say three kids," Anna asked.

"Yes," Millicent confirmed.

"Twin boys and a girl," Millicent and Anna spoke simultaneously.

Anna accepted Millicent's revelation. "Sarah's alive, but how?"

"I don't think we'll ever know considering the source," Gladys commented.

"It's about time we found out the truth. Furthermore, Sammy needs to pay for all the pain he's caused." Anna whizzed past Millicent and Gladys out the window.

"Wait," Gladys called out, but it was too late. Anna vanished into the night.

"Does she even know where he is?" Millicent wondered.

"She's determined, so she'll find him. I'm afraid of what will happen when she does, Small."

To take Gladys' mind off her qualms, Millicent switched the conversation to her progression. "I did come back with some good news. I remembered some things."

"That's wonderful!"

"I was married with two daughters. I only regained a few sketchy flashbacks of them, nothing else. I pray that they're well."

"I'm sure they are."

"Maybe, when I remember more, I can find them and be there for them in spirit-bird form."

Learned lessons overruled Gladys' compassion. "Will you be strong enough to handle that? Look at Sammy, if he's telling the truth. It's hard to accept a non-participatory role in a life story you created. Look at me. Look at Anna. My regret brought both of us here. If I knew then what I know now, I would've made a different choice."

This was as good a time as any for Millicent to get some more background information on Anna. What better way to find out about the daughter than to go through the mother. She started with an obvious observation.

"Gladys, is this house part of Anna's human life?"

"Yes, she shared this home with her family. I gave her up for adoption when she was born. I doubted my plan as soon as the eager nurse removed her from my arms. I was nineteen when I got pregnant. I was unstable. Her father skipped town before I could get out 'It's yours.' She deserved a better life than what I could give her, she never fully achieved it though. I searched for her when I got my cancer diagnosis. I wanted to clear my conscience and beg for forgiveness.

Millicent clung to Gladys' every word like an observant student.

"I found out she bounced from foster home to foster home. Some were tolerable but the others would have made my one room shack seem like paradise. I located Anna through a social worker who knew her from the work she did with homeless youth. By this time, she was all grown up. She lived here with her husband and daughter, who was around three-years-old at the time. I drove past this house so many times trying to get a glimpse into her life. They were such a happy family. Hey, come with me.

Gladys flew out of the window with Millicent behind her. They landed in front of the house where Gladys could point out the actual references to aid in the continuation of her story.

"I'd see all three of them playing in the front yard. Sometimes, I'd only see Anna and her daughter planting flowers in those beds." Gladys' right wing directed Millicent's eyes to the two overgrown flowerbeds flanking the walkway. "She was an attentive mother. I'm not sure where she picked up her motherly instincts." Gladys continued to use her wing like a pointer while she resumed her trip down memory lane. "I would leave my car at the park up the road, walk down this street, glance into that picture window and catch them on the couch watching TV, enjoying each other.

Without warning, Gladys flew to the sidewalk to take in the full view of the house. Millicent followed.

"On one of my walk-bys, Anna and my granddaughter were out front blowing bubbles. She greeted me with her father's big, beautiful smile. It was my mission to say hello every day after that in hopes of starting a dialogue. We never said more than hello." Remorse showed on Gladys' face. "I sensed she was never as happy again as she was on that day. A mother knows her child. I knew something was driving a wedge between her and her husband. Then her belly started to grow. Cancer won before I gathered the nerve to introduce myself. I guess God's plan is God's plan, but I had plans of my own. I wasn't there for my first grandchild's birth. I couldn't miss the second. I stepped out of the light because I didn't want to let go again.

Gladys took off with Millicent close behind her as they flew to the back of the house, landing on top of the pergola.

"I was the first bird to call this pergola home. I watched over them like a proud mother/mother-in-law/grandmother whose name they didn't know. I remember when they left for the hospital that morning. I darted off right with them. Determination allowed me to keep up with Brian's crazy driving. I circled every inch of that hospital looking for a way in. When that didn't work, I wandered the rooftop trying to decide my next move when I saw the light. It was bright and so familiar. Anna, with her newborn baby boy cradled in her arms, levitated into the sky in the light's clutch. She struggled with her reality. She didn't want to go. She kissed her son's forehead, gave him to God and freed herself from the light. I was there for her as I should've been in life. I told her who I was, and she didn't doubt my truth or curse my decisions. She was just thankful I was there at that moment. I was finally able to do what I should've done all those years ago. I brought my baby back home and we've been here ever since."

From the pergola, Gladys returned to the attic with Millicent.

"These are all her old things? How's her family doing? What about her daughter?" Millicent had questions about Anna's past that were similar to the questions she wanted answered regarding her own life. Gladys answered them one by one.

"Yes, these are all her things. Her husband moved on rather fast. He lives here now with his new wife, daughter and Anna's daughter. It depends on who you ask to get an answer on how my granddaughter is doing. She's physically fine, well fed, clothed and taken care of, but emotionally is a different story. Anna and I both agree her stepmother and father cleared all signs of Anna out of their everyday lives. Where we differ is whether it was on purpose. I don't think so. I feel her father and stepmother failed to realize how sacred the bond is between mother and child. Nothing should ever try to come between it, not even death. Humans are creatures of habit and make mistakes. I didn't realize the importance then either. I know now. The one good thing to come from our situation is our bird's eye view. We've become specialist at seeing the error of our ways and the ways of others. The bad thing is we can't do anything about it."

"So, her daughter is the future she's trying to protect." Millicent gained a better understanding of Anna's hypocrisy. "Do you think Anna's widower and new wife will ever see the error of their ways?"

Gladys looked at Millicent with a smile. "Humans make mistakes, but God has a way of offering them second chances. I'm sure all wrongs will be rectified, Small."

Millicent piggybacked on Gladys' hopefulness with a surprise of her own. "My name isn't Small, Gladys. It's Millicent, Millicent Hamilton."

"What!"

THIS ISN'T ME

Millicent and Gladys' facial expressions mirrored the comedy and tragedy masks, respectively. Gladys could not believe the strange twist of fate that brought her daughter's nemesis down to her level and at her doorstep. Ruin her recovery or remove more of Millicent's feathers were the questions that Gladys grappled with. Before making any foolish decisions, Gladys had to be certain.

"What did you say your name is?"

"Millicent Hamilton, why, do you know who I am, Gladys?"

The irony of Millicent unknowingly standing in the crypt of Anna and her past was overwhelming for Gladys. She was unable to decide anything on her own. "Um…um…I…but Anna…Anna, I have to tell Anna."

Gladys left out the window in a flash, leaving Millicent behind in the dark. The feelings of abandonment resurfaced for Millicent; however, she lost interest in that and found intrigue in the room she was left in. Furniture and containers adorned with thick layers of dust and the cobwebs in the corners made it apparent no one ventured up there that often. Millicent hopped around and found an open jewelry box tucked away in an obscure corner, void of dust. This suggested its placement on top of a couple of large storage boxes was recent. A shiny silver locket draped over one of the corners. Next to it was a picture of a woman holding a child. Fingerprints replaced the ink along the edges of the photograph as if the possessor held it tightly for as long as they could. Millicent stared at the photo of what she assumed was Anna's human image with her daughter and instinctively compared Anna's image to hers. Although Millicent admitted Anna was pretty, her confidence insisted she wasn't as attractive as the real image she saw of herself in the store window. Millicent's fixation ended with the sound of car doors.

"The family's here."

Millicent attempted the same dramatic departure out the attic window as her predecessors to see Anna's family, but she could barely shimmy her body out of the opening. Her new wings were sore from the pecking she received from Sammy. By the time she made it out the window, the garage door lowered shut. She snooped in on the living room. The lights were on; disappointingly, no one appeared in sight. A second-floor window showed light and movement. There was a picture frame on the floor. The frame's glass was shattered making the photograph unrecognizable. Millicent moved around trying to spot someone inside, but a trellis engulfed by an overgrown rose bush obstructed her view. She maneuvered through the thorns to get a better look only to abort her mission after hearing the cautionary siren of bees behind her. She escaped to window number two at the rear of the home above the pergola. It happened to be open so Millicent invited herself in to investigate. There were butterfly murals on the wall, dolls and a tea set in the corner. This was the bedroom of the youngest daughter.

The room's owner entered, cut on the lights and closed the door. Millicent hid in between a picture frame. The little girl, dressed in pink unicorn pajamas, took a fuzzy teddy bear from her bookcase, turned off the light and climbed into bed. Millicent resurfaced from behind the kickstand of the frame. Her noiseless exit foiled when her tail feather swiped the kickstand and caused the picture frame to fall backwards. In response to the commotion, the child reached up and turned on her desk lamp. The discovery of the picture inside the frame conquered

Millicent's initial reaction to flee. It was her human image. The sight of herself in the picture unlocked the rest of Millicent's brain. "The man is Brian, my husband. Next to him is Bri, my stepdaughter. Brian's her father and her mother is...her mother is...." Millicent struggled with the name of Brianna's mother. "That's the same little girl in the unicorn pajamas. She's my daughter, Penny. I'm in her room. Wait...wait...wait... the pergola, the birds, the disrepair, this is my house. The attic, that old photo, I remember her. I drove myself crazy trying to be her. I've lived in that woman's shadow my entire marriage. It's Bri's mother, Mari...Marianna...Mari...Anna...Anna...Anna and Gladys.... Gladys, she does know me."

"Little birdie, why are you keeping up so much noise?" Penny sat at her desk. "I guess you want me to finish my story. I knew you'd be back. That's why I opened the window for you. My family doesn't think I should be talking to you, but I know you like my stories. That's why you keep coming back." Penny picked up the frame and started from where she left off. "So, you know this is my family. My mommy's right here." Penny pointed to Millicent's real image. "She was in an accident this morning. She's in a comma...I mean a coma. She's going to get better because we were at the hospital and Nana felt her squeeze her hand so that means she's going to wake up. I hope it's soon because I really, really miss her." A tear rolled down Penny's cheek as Millicent watched helpless. "I'm sorry birdie," Penny apologized as more tears rolled down her cheeks. "I can't talk anymore. I'll see you in the morning and we can talk again like we always do." Penny signaled Millicent to take a ride on her finger. She escorted her mother outside, let her down with care, then closed the window, turned off the lamp and climbed back into bed.

"All this time she's been interacting with those birds not knowing one day her kindness would help her own mother.

My lucky Penny, but is she right. I'm in a coma, not dead."

The door to Penny's room opened. Millicent pressed her face into the windowpane to see who was interrupting her daughter's sleep. It was Brianna.

I wonder what she wants. Probably came to rub it in my baby's face that I'm in the hospital. I guess she gets her vindictiveness from Mari.

"Penny, are you asleep?"

Penny rolled over in her bed toward the sound of her sister's voice. "No, I'm not sleep yet."

Brianna noticed her little sister's red, watery eyes. "Have you been crying?" She settled herself on the bed.

A child overcome with adult emotions, Penny hurled herself onto Brianna and cried into her shoulder. "I'm scared Bri. I don't want my mommy to die. I don't want to be like you. You're mean and bad all the time because your mother isn't here. I don't want to be bad. I don't want to be like you. I want my mommy!"

The pane of glass on Penny's bedroom window wasn't thick enough to mute her cries as Millicent listened in. *My poor baby, do something Bri.*

Repentance and dread took the form of tears and washed over Brianna's face. For Penny's sake, she knew she had to turn her pain into strength. She inhaled a deep breath, wiped away her fleeing teardrops, and reminded Penny of the promise she made to her earlier. "Hush little Sis, I told you Mom is going to be fine, didn't I?"

She called me Mom.

"Besides, I'm here so there's no way I'm letting you make the same bad decisions I made. You're going to stay a good girl and I'm going to be a better big sister. I'm going to listen to Mom and I'm not going to be a bad girl anymore. Everything is going to be OK."

"Isn't that what Nana told you and it wasn't," Penny mumbled, still with her head buried in Brianna's shoulder.

"What if you're lying to me like Nana lied to you? What if you're being an adult?"

"Well, if you don't believe me," Brianna lifted Penny's head up and looked into her flooded eyes. "What about God? God answers prayers, so let's pray."

Brianna evicted herself from Penny's embrace, placed the child on her feet by the bed, kneeled down on the floor and motioned to her sister to follow her lead.

"No, we need to make sure God hears us." Penny cleared space on her desk, climbed on top and opened the window. Millicent shuffled to the side and used the night as her camouflage. Brianna joined her sister on top of the desk. They both got on their knees in front of the window, and Brianna started the prayer.

"Dear God, please wake our mom from her coma and make our family complete again. We need her Lord. We love her; even though we might not show it, we also really, really appreciate her and want her back home. I promise to stop driving her crazy—"

"I'll be good too, God. I'll stop getting into things that don't belong to me, and I'll stop standing on the furniture. I'll start that after we pray," Penny added.

Brianna finishes, "Please heal her God, Amen."

"Amen," Penny ended.

They placed their woes in God's hands. Brianna closed and locked the window. Millicent returned to her front row view in time to see Brianna put Penny to bed. Brianna pulled the covers up, kissed the palms of Penny's hands and whispered in her ear. That brought a big smile to Penny's face. She found her perfect sleeping position and closed her eyes. The room went black.

Millicent watched, until all she saw was her own reflection. "I never knew birds could cry." With that said, Millicent extracted the most significant recollection. She wasn't a bird. "If I'm not dead, there has to be a way for me to become human again. Anna has to know something, but why would Mari or Gladys help me? They're the ones who inflicted this eternal punishment. I need Sammy's help."

A SECOND CHANCE

Brianna crouched against Penny's door. Her head was laden with contemplations of if she made the same mistake her dad and grandmother made with her nine years ago by giving premature hope to her little sister in order to pacify her fear. Was she too much of a grownup? Her eyes no longer welcomed moisture. It was time to get comfort. At the end of the hall were the attic stairs. Brianna climbed up and turned on the light to her past. Her course was straight to her mother's vanity. She opened a drawer, pulled out a half-emptied bottle of perfume, sprayed the fragrance in the air and caught the loose droplets with her hands. She reached into a crate and retrieved a family album. Thumbing through the pictures made her smile.

"Bri, are you up here?" Valerie's head popped up among the items in the attic.

"I'm over here Nana. What are you doing up here?"

"You weren't in your room. I saw the stairs down, so I hoped it was you and not a burglar. Why are you up here?"

"Nana, if Dad and I let all this stuff go, will that make things better around here?"

Valerie knocked the dust off a footstool before taking a seat. "These things aren't the problem, Sweetie."

"Well what is? Is it me? Do I need to move out so they can be a happy family?"

"You're part of this family and this family's happiness depends on the happiness of each individual member. Getting rid of these things won't make matters better like keeping them locked up won't."

"Well Nana, what's the answer?"

"Light," Valerie replied.

"What?" Brianna was confused.

"Light, Honey. We covered up your mother and brother's deaths and treated them like a shameful secret. They didn't deserve that or this." Valerie's hands spanned the stacked boxes surrounding them. "It was no one's intention to act like they never existed. We didn't collectively decide it, but I know we all convinced ourselves not talking about it would lessen the pain. Instead, it compounded it and not just in your case. We've all suffered from our silence, but I'm sure Dr. Miller can help us with that."

"I don't think Dr. Miller's a good fit." Brianna reminisced back to her last encounter with Dr. Miller. "Can we research another therapist?"

"Sure, as long as we stay committed to seeking therapy. In the meantime, this vanity would look great in your bedroom. I think it's time we move some of these things out of the darkness and back with the living. Agreed?"

"Agreed!" Brianna gave her grandmother a hug.

The two selected other items from the attic they believed would be useful elsewhere. They carefully carried the vanity down the stairs and placed it along a bare wall in Brianna's room where she mingled her cosmetics with her mother's hair clips and accessories. They returned to the attic for other keepsakes like pictures, old clothes that cycled back in style and a chest of drawers Valerie felt would be an excellent solution for linen storage in the hallway. Once their makeover of the second floor was completed, they went downstairs and scattered pictures of Mari amongst the other family photos in the living room.

"What about this picture, Nana? Do you think it's too much?" Brianna pulled a twelve by twelve-inch framed wedding day portrait of Brian and Mari and handed it to Valerie.

"What a beautiful picture." Valerie sat the frame on the

mantle beside the wedding picture of Millicent and Brian.

"Nana, I know why we're doing this, but do you think Millicent will approve?"

"It'll be fine Bri. I can't think of a better representation of the love that brought you to this earth. Millicent has no reason to feel threatened by your mother. She'll understand." Valerie took a seat on the couch. "That's enough labor for tonight. We'll make a plan to get your Dad to help us bring more things down later."

Brianna took a seat next to Valerie and laid her head on her grandmother's shoulder. "Thank you, Nana."

****

Mindless chatter and song blasted through the branches of the oak tree. Since they didn't have the club's music, the birds decided to entertain themselves with their own renditions of crowd-pleasing ballads. From Hip-Hop to Country, it was like a stream of top forty hits playing altogether. It was an explosion of emotions, perfect backdrop for an unstable sparrow.

"Hey Sammy, you got company." A male's voice gave warning to an intoxicated Sammy.

"I knew you would be back," Sammy swiveled around to greet his anticipated visitor. He got Anna instead. "Anna, what are you doing here?"

"I'm here to get answers Samuel Rece. First, why did you attack the Small? Second, where are you hiding Sarah?"

Sammy, stunned that Anna would dare mention his wife's name since he blamed her preaching for turning Sarah against him, took a defensive stance. "You already overstayed your welcome. You need to leave if you know what's good for you."

"What, are you going to attack me too? I wish you were

stupid enough to make that mistake." Anna bellied up to Sammy and welcomed the long-awaited battle. "You don't have to worry about the first question. I know the answer, you're a sick psycho. But, you will tell me where Sarah is." Anna was so close she could smell the trepidation permeating from his pores.

Sammy let go of his tough guy routine in the presence of a formidable adversary. "She's alive and well, living her forever after with my best friend and our kid's godfather."

"Liar!" Anna lunged at Sammy piercing his body repeatedly with her sharp beak to give him a taste of his own medicine.

"Stop, I'm telling the truth! She's alive. I can show you proof. Stop and I'll show you proof. Please, stop!"

Anna granted Sammy's wish. "Don't play with me Sammy."

Sammy flew to the top of the convenience store with Anna on his tail in case he tried to make a run for it. He escorted her to a corner of the roof littered with trash and newspapers in the form of a makeshift domicile. He went inside while Anna stuck around on guard outside. Sammy reappeared from his lair dragging a piece of crumpled, yellowed newspaper with the front-page headline, "Local Woman Finally Wakens from Coma." He laid it out in front of Anna.

"You still know how to read, don't you?"

The more Anna read the more her eyes grew. She soaked the article in like a sponge over a spilled glass of water before concluding, "It's a miracle, but how?"

"She never died. I guess her soul was somehow separated from her body."

"Then are we…."

"No, we're long since digested maggot food. I suspect it's connected to the memory loss. Smalls must be in some kind of suspended state like a coma. When Sarah started to remember, she kept telling me she wasn't dead. I would tell her to shut up and deal with it, but she kept insisting she wasn't dead. I guess she sensed it. Of course, I didn't believe she wasn't and wanted to prove to her that she was deceased. One day I took her to our family burial plots so she could see our tombstones. We only found mine. The ground adjacent to me, her plot, was undisturbed. That's when I believed her."

"But how did she become whole again?"

"When we discovered the truth, she was determined to find her body. I'd never seen that much fight in her before. She led the way to the most logical place, Calverton Memorial. We canvassed that hospital from top to bottom, peeked in every window, until we found her. Believe me when I tell you there was a strong, magnetic force filling that room. I felt the suction from outside. It had to be pure luck that someone left a window in her room open. Sarah flew in through that opened window and I saw her be reborn. It was miraculous. After that day, I kept up with her new life until my heart couldn't anymore."

"Wow, I didn't know you had a heart."

Furious Anna would turn a sensitive moment into a joke, Sammy fired back. "I'll be sure to ask you how your heart feels once your friend, the Small, reunites with her body. Why am I calling her Small? She remembered her name. What did she say it was? Oh yeah, it's Millicent Hamilton. You know Millicent Hamilton, don't you," he asked with his signature devilish smirk.

"She can't be!"

"She is, Honey," Gladys intervened. "She told me after I opened up to her about you, me and our connection to the house. She's regained some of her memory, but she hasn't figured out she's part of our equation."

"Penny did say she was in an accident and that she was sleeping, but how do we know Millicent's like Sarah?"

Anna looked to Sammy for the answer.

Sammy motioned Anna and Gladys to follow him. He led the women to a single copy newsstand located in the front of the store. He watched as their eyes moved from left to right reading the headline, "Prominent Businesswoman in Coma Following Yesterday's Car Accident," below that was a photo of Millicent.

"Ladies, I can't say I enjoyed this late-night visit, but would you be so kind to leave me alone. If I don't get some sleep, I'll be cranky and unbearable all day. Please give Millicent my best." Sammy retired to his paper cave.

"What does this have to do with Sarah, Anna?"

"We need to go to Calverton Memorial. I'll explain everything on the way."

****

Anna and Gladys arrived at Calverton Memorial with Gladys up to speed on what was going on. They searched the rooms, spied in every window, until they reached the third floor. There, they spotted Millicent in the hospital bed with Brian by her side, connected by ring fingers.

"See, it's true Gladys."

"I can't believe it. I don't trust Sammy. I don't believe it."

"I read the article Gladys, Sarah's alive."

Gladys still needed convincing. "But that light came down on all of us. We were headed for heaven."

"The light came down for Sammy too," Anna remarked. "Do you really think he was going to heaven?"

"What about Tasha Roberts and Eric Smitie," Gladys referenced. "They both came in as Smalls, both regained their memory, both are still sparrows, both are still dead. Explain that?"

"What about the other Smalls we've come across over

the years that seemed to sporadically disappear? You explain that. We didn't stay with the light, we don't know for sure what was on the other side. What if it was life but we gave up by accepting death. Sarah's life with Sammy was already hell on Earth. She knew it couldn't be her eternity. She never accepted death. She fought for her life and got a second chance as her reward. We dismissed fate to take matters in our own hands, and look at what happened." Anna brandished her wings to emphasize her point.

"Maybe you're right. Our selfishness blinded us so that we couldn't see the miracle. We need to help Millicent find her way back."

Anna focused on Brian holding Millicent's hand. "For once it's not about her." Anna looked at Gladys. "Do you feel that? I can feel the force pulling. It's the energy from a body desperately seeking a soul," Anna visualized a plan and concluded, "any soul."

"Anna no, that vessel is not yours. You cannot take the place of Millicent."

"Why not, she didn't mind taking my place."

"She didn't, Anna. No one can take the place of a loved one departed or otherwise, only ease the pain. You of all people should know that to be true. You never knew me in life, but you always had forgiveness in your heart for the decision I made. You never let anyone try to take my place; therefore, you shouldn't try to take the place of Millicent. You've already left your legacy."

"My legacy is calling another woman Mom while my things are banished to a dusty, smelly attic."

"My love, let Millicent's fate be hers and yours be yours. Remember what we were saying earlier about being selfish."

"Maybe I can work on that in my next life." Anna saw an opening in the wall of windows as her opportunity to prove the validity of Sammy's story. Unfortunately, for Anna, the draft caught the attention of a night nurse who closed the window before she could proceed with her plan. "Damn! The family should be back later this morning. I'll trail the car and make sure someone opens that window. In the meantime, we have to help Millicent."

"Oh good Anna, you've changed your mind."

"Of course not, we have to give her hope. We can't have her turn out like Tasha and Eric. They lost hope, stopped believing and became stuck in this world. Maybe it was my preaching that caused it. Anyway, we have to make sure Millicent continues to fight. She'll just be fighting for me. Let's get back to the house to make sure she doesn't gain full recollection." Anna gave the windows a last surveillance then headed home with Gladys.

"You see Millicent, I'm the only friend you got." Sammy and Millicent emerged from behind the shadows after overhearing the end of Anna & Gladys' conversation.

"Mari wants my life, well let's see if she gets it. What do I do now, Sammy?"

"We have to make sure it's you that gets into that hospital room. We need to get you back home first."

"Why not stay here? Someone's bound to open a window sooner or later and I'll already be in position."

"Anna and Gladys don't know you have your full memory, we need to keep it that way. If you're not at the house, they'll get suspicious and come back here. Neither one of us is in any condition to stand up to Anna now."

"Are you sure this is the only way for me to return to my body? How do you know it's even going to work?

Not prepared for Millicent's second-guessing, Sammy had to concoct a response, "I felt bad for not being there for you as you regained your memory. I wasn't being a good friend, but now I want to help. When you told me your connection to Anna and that you weren't dead, I remembered something I overheard from the crows. They said this is what you have to do."

"The crows told you, how did Anna find out?" Millicent's sharp intuition tested Sammy's quick thinking.

"I guess she talked to them too, maybe yesterday, last week or last month when she planned this whole thing. I don't know."

"But Anna wouldn't talk to the crows."

"Why, because that's what she told you? Open your eyes to what's around you Small, Anna's your enemy! You're standing here doubting me, when she kicked you out of the light. She wants to take your life, leaving you stuck as a sparrow forever, yet you still trust her?"

"I can't let her take my life."

"Right, so let's go."

Millicent was reluctant to part ways. The attraction was undeniably strong. Seeing Brian holding her hand brought back the memory of when he first asked her to marry him. She said no because she wanted to pursue her dreams uninterrupted. Marriage eventually led to a carriage and at the time, her professional ambition outweighed the maternal. Millicent thought she would never feel Brian's touch again, she did. When he slid that gold band on her finger and vowed for better or worse, through sickness and in health, this moment proved that he meant every word. All the doubts and the arguments seemed so asinine at this point.

"I love you, Brian." Millicent left in Sammy's direction, going against her better judgment once again.

****

Anna patrolled the length of the concrete patio slab wondering where Millicent was and how to enact her plan. "Where is she?"

"I left her in the attic."

"She doesn't need to be in the attic, Gladys. She may remember everything. We need to keep her out the loop at least until I get into that hospital room. You can tell her whatever you want after that."

"If I were the jealous type, I would ask what's so bad about living here with me."

Gladys sought empathy; to her surprise, Anna showed no sympathy in her response, "Gladys, this isn't living. What I've experienced as a sparrow is torture. Now that I know I can be released, nothing will deter me from the relief of this heartache."

"And what about the pain you'll be causing Millicent?"

"I didn't do this to her. She made the choice, like all of us, to leave the light so she can suffer the consequences."

"But you're taking away this choice from her—"

"Enough, Gladys! I said nothing remember, nothing."

Anna and Gladys flew back into the attic where they found Millicent. She was by the opened jewelry box with the silver necklace draped over one side. The photo; however, was removed. Sammy stayed tucked away, still close enough to ensure Millicent stayed on course with their plan.

"Hello, Small, wait, your name is Millicent. Gladys told me you've regained partial memory. Have you made any more progress?"

"Nope, there's nothing more to reveal."

"Did you have a chance to look around," Gladys suggested. "Something might jog your memory."

"That's unnecessary. There's nothing here that would make her remember anything Gladys, just abandoned junk and memories long forgotten."

"It's funny; though, how one person's junk can be another's lifeline," Gladys noted.

Straying from Sammy's script, Millicent wanted to get

the one question answered that plagued her all day. "Anna, why haven't you moved on?"

"This is my home Small, and it's in desperate need of repair. When you first met me, you called me a Fixer. I guess you were right, it's my job to fix my family."

"Life can offer you a second chance; however, the outcome doesn't always change in your favor or at all. Besides, what could you fix around here," Millicent made the observation with knowledge of Anna's plan in the forefront of her mind. "I mean considering you're a bird and not fit to lift a hammer or a paintbrush."

"It's more than cosmetic, Small. A new fence, a new coat of paint, that's all a mask, a front, while the heart is barely beating. This house suffered a tragic loss, yet instead of properly grieving, it rejoiced in a new doormat." The use of the word doormat was a clever and calculated pun. Anna got a dig in while avoiding any details she believed would aid in Millicent completely regaining her memory. "It's new and pretty but it's only there to do its job. It just wants to be a doormat. It has cute swirls instead of the traditional welcome because it knows it doesn't accept everyone. It has channels and grooves so the dirt and mud can wash off because it can't handle the heavy stuff; therefore, keeping the precious doormat seemingly perfect for everyone to admire. It even tried to convince my family that everything was all better and all they needed in their lives were clean feet."

"First, it's Millicent Hamilton," Millicent's ego demanded proper respect but she had to be committed to her and Sammy's plan and keep up the amnesia act. "Second, I happen to notice the doormat is still here so the family must love it. Maybe it's your ex-husband's favorite. How do you know that everything isn't all good?"

Anna stood toe to toe with Millicent in her crosshairs. "I witness everything the doormat doesn't care to see."

Millicent was unbothered by Anna's intimidation tactic. "Like what?"

"I see my daughter and her stepsister tormenting each other."

"When they returned a few moments ago, I saw them praying for their mother to get better. They were getting along so well the oldest, your child I assume, kissed the inside of her sister's hands." Anna appeared more alert when Millicent mentioned that fact. "Someone must be making a positive impact on them. I mean, your child wouldn't call a woman she hated mother."

Anna didn't care if what she was about to say caused Millicent to remember everything, she wasn't sparing feelings and countered with, "Well, I've seen my daughter cursing her stepmother and wishing she were dead. The little one tells me how much she hates her mother for being so mean to her daddy. Let's not forget my widower. I see his long gazes into nowhere after an argument with his wife, maybe he hopes for a way out of a marriage that happened out of convenience. He needed a female figure around for our daughter. His choice happened to become pregnant and finally trapped him, but he still holds on to these treasures in the attic. On days when he really needs to escape her nagging, he comes up here to smoke. He keeps a pack of cigarettes, matches and a can of air freshener beside the bookcase in the corner. He hangs out of the window puffing his sorrows away. He hasn't smoked since his freshman year of college. That doesn't seem like a positive influence to me."

Check

Millicent, covered in denial, couldn't stand losing another fight to Anna. "All families have their moments of frustrations; fortunately, those storms do pass."

"Moments but not years, Millicent. At some point you have to ask yourself are you weathering the storms, or are you causing them."

and mate.

Millicent had no words as Anna's winning statement placed her in deep concentration. "Excuse me." Anna cleared the path and Millicent exited the attic the way she first came in—defeated.

"Anna, what have you done," Gladys chastised her daughter.

"She had to hear the truth."

"Yes Anna, and your truth might set her free."

Gladys' words reminded Anna of what she didn't want to happen. "Oh no!" Anna fled the attic wishing her bluntness didn't cause Millicent to abandon hope.

Millicent walked the roof's peak like a ship's plank and spouted her inner thoughts aloud, "All I've ever tried to do is take care of my family and make them happy. Why does their unhappiness have to be my fault? What stress could Brian be under to make him start smoking again? He hasn't done anything for the past six months. After all I've done, all I've given, all I've withheld from her father, that teenage terror wished I were dead! My own flesh and blood hates me because I want her father to have accountability twenty-four-seven, not just during halftime. Maybe I'm so mean because I'm holding this whole family arena on my back. I can't see the game, can't play in it, and the only feedback I get from my darling family is grief about how far back the seats are. I've let them get away with their ungratefulness for too long. Their DNA is imbedded with blame everything on Millicent. They wouldn't be able to change if they wanted to, and that's not my fault! It's not my fault! Is it my fault?

Millicent sat on top of the A-framed roof looking over the edge and analyzing the new memories of her past mistakes. The questions raised couldn't be overlooked and casted doubt on her innocence. "I'm the self-proclaimed hero who wreaks havoc as a villain only to become a hero again to clean up the mess I made. They don't know whether to love me or hate me. Maybe I should accept this punishment. Maybe it's time I focus on my new life, as a bird."

****

Daylight intruded through the hospital room like a prowler. The monitors that tethered Millicent's body like a marionette doll woke up and blasted off distress beeps. In his usual groggy morning voice Brian grumbled, "Millicent, turn off that dang...that alarm." Realizing he wasn't in his bed at home, Brian jumped out of his chairs screaming, "Nurse!"

A nurse ran into the room and attended to Millicent.

"What's going on," Brian asked as another nurse walked in.

"Mr. Hamilton, we need to ask you to leave," Nurse One said.

Brian was a brick wall. "I'm not moving. That's my wife and I need you to tell me what's happening to her?"

Nurse One explained, "Mr. Hamilton, that's what we are trying to ascertain. In order to do so, we need you to wait outside."

"Dr. Jones is on his way. She's in good hands, Mr. Hamilton. Please, allow us room to do our jobs," Nurse Two begged as she tried to back Brian out of the room.

Brian ignored the monitors and pleas from the nurses. He stood his ground and made a jaw-dropping confession to his wife, "I held a grudge. I never forgave you for saying no when I first proposed. I blamed you for my heartache then. If it wasn't for you, I wouldn't have met and lost Mari." Brian let out a deep sigh, "I blamed you for that pain too." Brian stiff-armed his way around Nurse

Two and walked to his wife. "There, I said what I've been holding in all these years. Are you satisfied? Now will you stop with the games! Get up so we can go home and be with our kids."

Finally revealing a major source of tension in their relationship should be enough to call off her convoluted prank, but Millicent didn't flinch nor did her tethers become quiet. Unconvinced, Brian placed his hands on his wife and shook her with half the weight of his personal shame, torment and frustration.

"Mr. Hamilton, please!" Nurse One planted herself in between Brian and the bed.

"Wake up Millicent, wake up," Brian shouted.

"Mr. Hamilton, do I need to call security and have you escorted out," Dr. Jones scolded as he entered the room. "I know this is an extremely difficult time for you, I sympathize, but I will not risk my nurses or my patient's wellbeing for your outbursts."

"Doctor, what's happening with my wife?"

"That's what I'm here to find out. Now please Mr. Hamilton, leave and let us save your wife!"

Nurse Two was successful in expelling Brian from the room and sped other hospital staffers in with their medical devices. Brian had to stand by. Millicent's life was no longer in his hands.

WHY

The sun barely had a chance to kiss the sky good morning before Valerie was downstairs making breakfast. There was a learning curve to navigate around with the modern kitchen appliances. Nonetheless, Valerie was satisfied with the health conscious meal she prepared. The girls arrived at the table, without coercion, anxious to eat and be back with their dad and mom.

"Good morning girls. As soon as we finish breakfast, I'll call your father to pick us up and take us back to the hospital."

"Nana, where's breakfast," Brianna asked.

"Right there in front of you," Valerie replied as she took her seat at the table. "We have a big bowl of oatmeal and fruit with toast on the side. Eat up."

"This doesn't look like the French toast Mommy makes," Penny explained. "Where's the whip cream smiley faces?"

"It's not French toast, its plain toast, Penny."

"But the calendar says it's French Day Thursday." Penny pointed to the family calendar on the front of the refrigerator. "We always have banana French toast with whip cream smiley faces on French Day Thursday." Penny ended with a pout accompanied by folded arms in protest.

"We also have meat from something that's oinked, mooed or clucked," Brianna interjected.

"Too much meat isn't good for you, Bri."

"Nana, no offense—"

"That's usually what someone says when they are about to say something offensive so tread lightly, Bri."

"We're growing, active kids. We can handle meat, fat and sweets. This is old people's food. Millicent's no world-renowned chef; still, her breakfasts are much better than this."

"Wow, so let me get this straight. Millicent wakes up, gets herself ready, makes an elaborate themed breakfast for the family, eats and heads off to her high-profile job while you all do what exactly?"

"It's summer break so pretty much watch TV, play video games and hang out with friends."

"Or play with Daddy," Penny cracked.

"Play with your father? He's starting a new business; he shouldn't have time to play around."

"That's what Mommy says, but he finds a way." Penny shrugged her shoulders and sipped some of her juice before continuing. "We go to the arcades, the movies, the mall and even out for pizza. Can I have pizza for breakfast?"

"No you cannot, Penny. It seems like your father wants to be a child himself."

"He's the laidback one and Millicent's the strict one. Although," Brianna looked to Penny for confirmation. "If we push back, she usually ends up doing what she tried to make us do."

The girls allowed their mischievous smiles to escape. Valerie was not amused.

"I guess I'm the old school one. You two are going to eat the meal I've prepared and enjoy it. After that, I want you to clean and put away the dishes, then go up to your rooms and tidy up until your father gets here."

"Yes, Nana," Brianna and Penny responded together, neither one brave enough to show any resistance to their grandmother.

****

Anna found Millicent sitting on the edge of the roof's peak experiencing the breakthrough of a new day. "There you are Millicent, thinking about jumping to your death? It wouldn't work because you can fly." Anna nudged Millicent and laughed as if they were best friends.

"I never imagined being side by side with you," Millicent said. "I made up so many test, so many questions to prove you weren't all that to burst the bubble you left in my husband and mother-in-law's minds. Since you're here, I've narrowed it to one question. What would you do differently?"

"What," Anna, taken aback, said.

"I know it's you Marianna. I remember everything. I also know about your plan which is why I'm asking why you think you're better for my family than me?"

****

Brian's matted footprints dulled the freshly buffed tiles in the waiting area. His thoughts trespassed upon by everything from Millicent, the girls, Valerie to his own health. Nonetheless, a new day came with a new attitude. As he treaded the square footage, Brian chanted to calm his nerves, "Millicent has to wake up. She has to survive this. Millicent's going to wake up. She has to make it through this."

"Mr. Hamilton, are you OK?" Dr. Miller approached Brian, concerned with his present state.

"Doctor…." Absentmindedness took over Brian's brain.

Dr. Miller gave Brian a reminder, "Miller."

"Yes, Dr. Miller. I'm not good, neither is Millicent. There are monitors beeping, nurses all around, I have no clue what's going on. They forced me out here. I don't have time to talk doctor; I need to get back in there with my wife."

Brian tried to make his way back behind the double doors; no luck, Dr. Miller stopped him with gentle hand-to-hand contact.

"Mr. Hamilton, I know Millicent is in the best of care. She's going to be OK."

"Dr. Miller, in the past few days I've learned I can't always trust that statement."

"You have to believe that she is going to pull through. You should never give up," Dr. Miller imparted, "especially when the circumstances are this great."

"I believed that with my first wife Mari only to see her and our newborn son die in this same hospital. I said Bri would be OK if I blocked her from all the bad memories of our past but it destroyed our relationship. I said my marriage to Millicent would be OK and look where we are. The pain is starting all over again. What I'm trying to say doctor is saying everything is OK doesn't make anything OK!"

"You're right Mr. Hamilton, simply saying it doesn't. It's the strong belief, the faith, the action you put into those words, no matter the outcome, that makes the statement true. You can live through your pain or you can pack it all away and act like it doesn't exist."

"I know where the latter gets you. Dr. Miller, I need you to help my family live."

"It would be my pleasure, Mr. Hamilton?"

"Thank you, and please call me Brian."

"You're welcome Brian, and you can call me Sarah."

****

Even after remembering who she was, Anna was astonished at the level of disrespect Millicent showed in her presence. "Your family, Brianna is my daughter and Brian was the love of my life. I finally felt my luck changed for the better when I met him. I knew we were going to have a fairytale life together." Anna laughed at her idealistic future. "We even had a fairytale themed wedding."

"I know. I received the invitation in the mail." *The worst day of my life.*

"He sent you one even after I told him I didn't think it was a good idea." Anna joined Millicent for a seat on the rooftop. "I guess I have always lived in your shadows. I assumed it would be different after we got married, had Brianna, and it was. It was wonderful. Soon after, your father passed and Brian had to reach out to you. I'll admit I wasn't thrilled. Valerie warned me about your possessive nature over Brian; nevertheless, I knew the man who I exchanged vows with wouldn't betray me."

"It was not betrayal, Mari. I never—"

Anna didn't want to listen to excuses. She had some things to get off her chest. "Then your mother died, which made the phone calls between the two of you more frequent. He didn't sneak around to do it. I knew every time you called, every time he returned your call, every joke he told to make you laugh and vice versa. At that point, I saw things beginning to change between him and me. Brianna was no longer the cute baby who made us gush. She was a toddler with an independent spirit and attitude. I figured having another child would put his attention back on his family, I was wrong. I knew he would go to you. I didn't expect it to be so soon, neither did I ever expect your union to be a negative impact on Brianna. How could someone who experienced extreme losses not know how to comfort a child going through the same thing?" Anna looked to Millicent before she provided her own answer, "Selfishness! You and Brian were selfish with your love. You finally got your happily ever after, only my daughter didn't fit your fairytale ending."

"Wait, Mari!" Millicent went from sitting to standing. "That's not true. I've always loved Bri as my own."

Anna matched Millicent's movements and stood firm on her critique. "As if she was your own," Anna repeated to show Millicent the error in her words. "She's not yours. Brianna is the result of Brian's and my love. I gave him his first child and you can't deal with it. You tolerate Brianna because she's an extension of Brian. You don't love her. How could you when you've tried to erase half of her?

"You asked why I think I'm better," Anna recounted Millicent's original question then disclosed, "it's because I know how to give unconditional love. I have the instincts to recognize when they're sad and need motherly advice and support, not coddling. I see my younger self in Brianna. It's not easy walking around with a giant hole in your soul filled with anger and confusion because a piece of you is missing. Thank God DHS eventually placed me with a foster mother that channeled me toward activism and volunteering. My baby has no one to invest in her interest, that's why she's acting out. It's a cry for help that you and Brian can't stop aggravating each other to notice and wipe her tears. Penny informed me you and Brian were going to the pastor to learn how to love each other better, yet you two weren't smart enough to figure out it might be a good idea to put grief counseling for Brianna on your agenda. It's as if everything is solely about you and Brian. You're out for self-happiness not making this family happy.

Millicent absorbed each word as Anna continued to berate her.

"The kissing of the palms you saw, I showed Brianna that. It meant that she would never have to feel alone or afraid, that she would always have love and protection in the palm of her hands. You and Brian made me out to be a liar. So don't tell me you love her. She lost the only one who loved her when they lowered my casket in the ground. I had to watch you two sharing clothes, acting like one of her girlfriends and making her call you Mom. You tried to remove the last strand that bonded me to my daughter and for what, you psycho. You were already there in person, but you wanted more. That's greed, that's control, a power play from the career professional not love."

Enough was enough for Millicent. "I guess you think if you say I'm a terrible mother and stepmother over and over again it will make it true, you're wrong. I'm not about to let you of all people stand in my face and stamp that label on me." Millicent showed no sign of weakness as she backed Anna down the pitch of the roof while she recited facts all the way, "Although you had a different perspective as a bird, you're still not seeing the full picture. I cook for her. I clean up after her. I help her with her homework. I go to all of her performances. I talk to her about being a woman. I was there when she got her first period and her first boyfriend. I taught her about the birds and the bees. I'm the ATM when she needs money for makeup and the chauffeur for her and her friends. I'm the one at every parent-teacher conference. I'm the one leaving work when she gets in trouble. She insists on fighting with the other girls at school because of the secret boyfriend. I'm the reason he's the secret ex-boyfriend. I proudly do more for Bri than her own father, so don't stand here and tell me I don't love that child. Yes, I've made mistakes with her, Penny and Brian, but I still love them all unconditionally. I haven't thrown in the towel; I can't, I won't despite what any outsider says."

"Neither have I!" Passion blazed in Anna's eyes as she pushed back with her words and backed Millicent up to their original resting position. "God got it wrong. It wasn't my time to die and this second chance is His way of answering my prayers and correcting His error. No coincidence I found and brought you here. God allowed me to watch and learn from your slip-ups over the years. Now, He's giving me the opportunity to take what's rightfully mine. It's finally time for me to come back inside my home."

"Back in your home, you batty bird, this is my house and the only way you will get back in is over my dead body."

Confidence surged through Millicent's veins. She gave Anna a hard push sending her rolling down the side of the roof, ending with her face down inside the gutter. Anna wasn't down long, she rushed back at Millicent feet first. Millicent tried to maneuver up to avoid impact but was too slow. Anna's scaly claws connected with Millicent's chest and she tossed her over the opposite side of the roof. Millicent sailed past the roof and landed on the shoulder of her husband.

"Brian babe, please save me from this lunatic!" Millicent hoped her bond with Brian would transcend the rules of the afterlife as she chirped into her beloved's ear.

"He can't hear or help you. I'm glad to see my love. He deserves to feel my wrath as much as you do."

Millicent used Brian's head as a shield to keep Anna at bay while Brian used his hands to prevent her from scratching his eyes out. Brian made his way over to the grill with Anna and Millicent buzzing around him like mosquitoes.

"Get over here, you crazy birds!" Brian opened the lid on the grill. "We'll be eating barbecue sparrows for dinner once I get my hands on you." Brian tried to snatch Anna and Millicent out of the sky. It was obvious he had the upper hand, forcing the lovers of his past and present to fly off, one behind the other.

****

Valerie relaxed on the sofa with her feet up on the upholstered coffee table while enjoying her second cup of Millicent's herbal tea. Although she preferred her eye-opening standard, roasted coffee, she couldn't hate on her daughter-in-law's choice. She sipped and flipped through a magazine waiting for Brian to return.

"We're done clearing the table and cleaning up the kitchen, Nana." Brianna notified her grandmother short-winded as if she and her sister returned from a sentence of hard labor.

"Good, you and Penny go straighten up your rooms until your dad arrives."

"Yes ma'am," Brianna and Penny panted as they walked to their bedrooms to continue their chores.

A loud commotion coming from the backyard interrupted Valerie's browsing. "Brian, is that you?" Valerie called out from the sofa to the sound of jingling keys coming from the kitchen area. Brian gave no reply. He walked past his mother, who made her way to the kitchen, and went to the hallway closet to retrieve a baseball bat. Ready for war, Brian passed his mother again without saying a word and headed back outside. Valerie stood in the middle of the kitchen with her hands up, her face showing the expression of the question she asked herself in her head. Not waiting for an answer, she walked out to investigate. Once in the backyard, she saw her son standing in the middle of the patio in a hitter's stance prepared to whack whatever thrown his way out of the park.

"Brian, what's going on?"

"It's these birds. Millicent wanted this pergola down; well, it's coming down today."

Brian struck one of the pillars with the bat. This rattled

the birds resting on the slats above; however, they didn't move. He aimed higher with the second and third hits causing the wooden slats to splinter to the ground along with leaves from the ivy plants. This sent the sparrows into a frenzied evacuation in search of a safer refuge. One bird was so startled it left behind an unpleasant present that plopped on Brian's shirt collar.

"Crap!"

Brian took his eyes off the disgusting excrement blob to look at his mother. Valerie, embarrassed for her son, looked in his exhausted eyes, then the poop, finally back at Brian. She extended her arms and offered herself as a place for Brian to rest his troubles. He dropped the bat, removed his soiled shirt and accepted his mother's warm embrace. Brian placed his head in her chest and let all his heavy emotions dribble onto his mother's blouse. They walked arm in arm to the wicker patio sofa for a seat.

"Brian, who are you out here fighting?"

"My short comings, my insecurities, my tears, myself...."

"We are going to get through this. It's going to be alright, Son."

The sound of that seven-letter word and its many synonyms, that was the family's go to response, made Brian cringe. "Ma, I don't know if anything will ever be alright again."

Brian's pessimism outweighed Valerie's optimism. His intentions were to break the news to his mother about Millicent's overnight decline in health, but instead of an update, he had questions, "Why do we plead for second chances? Why do we even bother with life at all?"

"Excuse me," Valerie sought further explanation from Brian.

"Look at Mari. She went through hell her entire childhood. She overcame that without an ounce of bitterness, found love, gave birth to Bri and right when we're starting to write the third chapter of our fairytale she's gone. What's the point? What's the point of living when we know death is inevitable?"

"What's the point? Listen to me Brian. Yes, life is full of ups and downs and some of us may experience more downs than ups, but you don't give up on life because it doesn't go the way you planned. You fight for what you want. Second, third or fourth chance, it doesn't matter, even if death is the outcome. You live every moment to the fullest with purpose and thanksgiving. You live for them." Valerie placed herself in the middle of her two grandkids who ventured out to the patio at the right moment, curious to see what was happening. She swathed her arms around their shoulders and squeezed them while facing Brian. "As parents, it's our responsibility to instill values, protect them, make long-lasting impressions and fill their lives with love that carries on after we're gone. I'll be the first to admit that we don't always get it right." Valerie looked at Brianna as a prime example. "This is the greatest reason why we live son, so we never die."

"What's going on here? Dad, why are there pieces of wood and leaves all over the patio?"

"And Daddy why are your breasts out," Penny asked with laughter. Her childish humor lightened the mood and gave everyone a smile. "I've never seen your heart before." Penny approached her father and used her small hand to examine the heart-shaped tattoo encircling two sets of angel wings on her dad's chest.

"Your father and I were talking."

"Is everything OK," Brianna asked.

"Yes, everything's al-ri-ght." Valerie finally tasted the distrust in that statement. She looked to Brian for any sign of disagreement. He didn't interject anything suggesting otherwise. "Girls, let's get ready to go back to the hospital."

The opportunity to have a frank sit down with his family to discuss Millicent's deteriorating status vanished with Valerie, Brianna and Penny. Brian didn't follow. He lowered his head. "Fix this. Tell me what to do to make everything better because I have no clue. Please bring Millicent back to us. If it's not in Your plan, please show me how to keep her memory, as well as Mari's, alive."

****

Millicent and Anna had to wrap-up their chase. Brian's return meant the family was preparing to go back to the hospital. Neither one wanted to botch their strategy. With Anna millimeters behind, Millicent plunged down to reverse her position. She planted her feet in Anna's back and forced her to the ground. Before Millicent could gain freedom, she had to make Anna confess to her plot of exchanging fates for her own selfish reasons.

"You were right Mari, it wasn't a coincidence you found me since you're the one that pushed me out of the light!"

"I never touched you when you were in the light. You were already a bird when we met."

Millicent applied more pressure to Anna to get her to tell the truth or her second death would be at the claws of wife number two. Sounds of distress saved Anna.

"He's tearing down the pergola!"

"Lets get out of here!"

"He's lost his mind!"

The sparrows from the patio exclaimed as they retreated to a safer shelter. Millicent released her hold on Anna, which ended their duel. They both circled back to the pergola to find the reason for the commotion.

"What is Brian doing? He loved that pergola. He built it to protect us from the summer heat," Anna recalled.

Anna and Millicent watched while Brian struck out. They also watched as Valerie came out and embraced her son. What came next was something Millicent never witnessed before.

"I didn't know Brian could cry," Anna cited. This was confirmation that Brian's crying was indeed a rare exhibition.

Millicent and Anna were all ears as Valerie comforted Brian. Their somber mood lifted when their daughters came outside. They edged closer for Brian's prayer. After he went inside, Anna and Millicent sentiments flared with the same salty mix of disappointment and fury.

"Why did you do this to me?"

"I told you Millicent, I didn't push you out of the light."

"If it wasn't you, it had to be Gladys. This has nothing to do with favor. You two plotted this from day one."

"You are insane?"

"Why did you withhold your identity? Why didn't you tell me your name was Marianna?"

"Anna is the name Gladys wanted me to have. It was her grandmother's name. The delivery nurse mocked it and suggested the change. 'Anna know who's going to want this baby with the plain name.' Marianna sounded prettier and hinted to an exotic heritage most adoptive parents were looking for at the time. Gladys agreed since she wasn't going to keep me anyway. Listen Millicent, I had nothing to do with your accident. I didn't learn who you were until a couple of hours ago. That's when I started plotting against you." Anna's admission made her embarrassed but not discouraged. "Gladys wanted no part of any of this. Ask her, she'll tell you the same thing. It's the truth, let's go ask her."

Asking Gladys wouldn't convince Millicent of their innocence. Gladys would say and do whatever to protect Anna. Millicent only entertained her suggestion because she still had a plan of her own to implement.

Anna and Millicent entered the attic through the small opening in the oval, etched glass window. Anna called out to Gladys, no answer. They went back to the box, no sign of Gladys. Millicent called out to her accomplice. Sammy didn't appear or answer back so Millicent tried again. "Sammy!"

"Why are you calling him?"

"He was hiding behind those boxes. He was going to help keep you and Gladys here while I hitched a ride back to the hospital."

"Unbelievable, after all he's done you still trust him over me? Did you ever wonder why he withheld the truth about Sarah all this time? You told him you remembered your name, did he bring you back here and tell you who you were?"

"No," Millicent responded.

"Why not, Sammy knew who lived here. Your name should've sparked some reaction out of him. If Sarah told him about Gladys being my mother, I'm positive she told him about my connection to this place. He would've loved the opportunity to tattle that information, yet he told you nothing. I'd bet anything he's the cause of all of this."

Millicent couldn't bypass Anna's point. Her suspicions began to change, but a muffled SOS curbed her and Anna's exchange.

"That's Gladys," Anna inferred, "Gladys, where are you?"

"I'm in the corner by the bookshelf, hurry!"

Anna and Millicent found Gladys bound, top to bottom, by the silver locket necklace. Anna tried to untangle her; however, the more she freed Gladys, the more she entangled herself. Millicent removed part of the chain threaded through Gladys' beak.

While gasping for air, Gladys was able to identify her

attacker. "Sammy did this. He's over there on the other side of the bookshelf."

Before Millicent reached Sammy's location, he bolted past her. "Sammy, wait!" Millicent's attempt to gain Sammy's attention was ignored as she watched him dash out the window. Before Millicent had a chance to join him and execute their plan, Sammy forced the window shut. He used his beak as a hammer and inserted pieces of twigs he held in his claws into the space around the window's hinges to insure its permanent closure. "What are you doing, this wasn't part of our plan?"

From the right side of the glass window, Sammy came clean, "No, but it's all part of my plan. Let me be candid, Millicent. When I caused that accident yesterday, I swear I didn't know it was you beforehand. I was trying to have some fun. It wasn't until after our fight that the wheels began to turn. I'm sorry my temper got out of hand, I never wanted to inflict more pain on you than I already had. I tried to keep you from remembering anything. That's why I took you away from this house. You could've had a clean slate as a sparrow. I didn't want your life at first. I wanted your companionship. I saw how loving you were toward your family. I wanted that, but you rejected me. Rejection is the story of my life, human and after, except with Sarah. She truly loved me unconditionally and I blew it. You'll be fine as a sparrow. You already have friends." Sammy punctuated his last sentence with his signature devious smile.

"I'm not a sparrow! I'm a woman, a wife and a mother!"

"Not anymore, Millicent," Sammy determined.

"Why would you do this Sammy? What did I ever do to you?"

"It's nothing against you." Ashamed, Sammy looked away. "I love, need and want my wife and kids back in my life. I treated Sarah horribly and put my family through so much hell. They didn't deserve that, but I can be a better human being. It's too lonely for me here. I want that love back and I know how to love them now. I'm going to love them," back to sharing eye contact, Sammy ended, "in any form."

"Sammy, there is no way I'm going to allow you to keep me trapped in this attic forever."

"You're absolutely correct, Millicent. I wouldn't dare have you go through that. I really do care about you all, which is why I'm going to give you the very thing your fearless leader always preached about, a chance to move on. I'm setting you, Gladys and Anna free."

Sammy flashed his smirk for one last time, gave Millicent a right-wing salute and left.

NEVER GIVE UP

Millicent tried with all her might to muster up enough strength to open the window but it wouldn't budge. The sound of four doors slamming and an engine starting distracted her from her failure. "It can't be too late." The window received one more push before Millicent returned to Anna and Gladys for pity.

"Where's Sammy," Anna addressed Millicent.

"He's heading to the hospital to steal my life," Millicent responded with watery eyes. "You were right. He was behind all of this, the accident, everything. He closed the window and I can't get it open. It's too late." Her tears poured out in higher quantities as she envisioned her second chance becoming Sammy's second chance.

"Millicent, don't give up hope or you'll be trapped forever," Gladys warned.

"I should give up. I'll be stuck in this form forever but at least Sammy doesn't win."

"What's that smell?" Anna sniffed the air and detected an odor of something burning.

The trio turned and saw smoke coming from behind the bookcase. Upon further inspection, they noticed a flaming book of matches resting on top of old newspaper clippings overflowing out of a metal wastebasket. Next to that, were bins full of stuffed animals. The smoke evolved from light to robust. Millicent, Anna and Gladys' survival skills kicked in.

"Grab onto the edge with your feet before the fire spills over onto the floor," Anna commanded Millicent and Gladys. They clamped on tight to the rim of the trashcan. "Lift," Anna ordered. They flapped non-stop to lift the basket from the ground.

"Where are we taking it, Anna," Millicent inquired.

"Out the window," Anna said to Millicent.

"I told you, it's closed," Millicent reminded Anna.

"With the weight of this trashcan, we can break through,"

"Anna Honey, the weight is what's worrying me," Gladys commented. "The can is too heavy and it's getting too hot. I don't think I can hang on much longer."

"Let's set it down for a second. I think I have an idea," Anna instructed.

They sat the can on a plastic bin marked wedding items. Anna retrieved the locket. She unhooked the clasp with her beak, strung the chain through the small handles on the sides of the trashcan and relocked the clasp.

"Here, grab this section of the chain that way we're elevated away from the heat," Anna directed Gladys and Millicent. Her new plan worked for the moment but the window seemed miles away. As the flames grew, the heat singed the trio's feathers and gave their feet an unsolicited black pedicure. "We're almost there. Ladies I need you to gather up as much strength as possible to drive this can through that window. Ready…set…go!"

The first impact made a crack down the middle of the pane.

"That was good," Anna praised. "Let's try again. This time I'll hold the chain while you two fly from the back wall and use your momentum to push the can through the window. Go take your places. Ready…set…go!"

The second hit granted the sparrows their freedom. Gladys and Millicent returned to holding the chain and helped Anna steer the fireball down on the grates of the outdoor grill. Before they shut the lid to smother the flames, Anna unfastened the necklace from the trashcan and twirled it around her body in mid-air.

Millicent was dumbfounded. "I can't believe we did it. We make a pretty good team."

"We do, but this is where our season ends," Anna said. "I have to beat Sammy to the hospital. Gladys, we need to go, Gladys!

Anna and Millicent discovered Gladys on her back in the grass, panting heavily.

"Gladys are you hurt?" Anna examined her mother.

"The heat was too much," Gladys exhaled. "I don't feel well."

"Gladys, we need to get to the hospital," Anna begged.

Anna and Millicent traded gazes. Millicent knew Anna would never leave her mother in this state. This was the break she needed.

"Ladies, I want to thank you for all your help but I have to get back to my life, and it will be a better life. Anna, I was listening. I promise to learn from my mistakes." With those final words, Millicent rocketed off.

"Gladys, where are you hurting?"

"My feet…no, my wings, it's my wings. I can't fly."

Anna sensed Gladys' insincerity. "You're lying. We need to leave. I can't miss my second chance."

Gladys rose to her feet. "Anna, let Millicent be Millicent."

"No, Millicent is trying to be me. They need me. I was the perfect wife and mother."

"Yes, and perfection does not exist on Earth. God brought you as far as he wanted you to go. Millicent still has a purpose to fulfill."

Speaking through her tears, Anna responded, "It's so hard to let go again."

"Trust me, I know, but God makes no mistakes. He gave us memory in exchange for flesh. It's time we both excuse the flesh and never let go of the memories." Gladys embraced her daughter.

Anna felt warmth under her mother's wings making her final decision more acceptable. "I won't be defeating death, but I can help Millicent defeat Sammy."

Gladys concurred, "Let's do it!"

I LOVE YOU ALWAYS

The Hamiltons parked in the hospital lot, exited the vehicle and walked side by side through the sliding automated entry doors like this was an everyday family outing. Once inside the elevator, everyone's attention keyed in on the changing numbers. The number three lit up, a bell sounded and the doors opened. The family stepped out two by two on their way to Millicent's room.

"Oh great, I forgot the blanket. Here Bri, take the keys and go get the blanket out of the back," Brian asked.

"Dad, we brought her blanket in yesterday," Brianna responded.

"It's not for Millicent, it's for me. It gets cold in here at night. Go please, and take your sister with you," Brian replied with an unnecessary forcefulness.

The two girls got back in the elevator.

"Brian, there's something you're not telling. What's wrong," Valerie inquired.

"Millicent's condition worsened last night. Her brain activity has slowed down significantly. She's no longer breathing on her own. I wanted to tell you all at home, but I couldn't."

"Brian, is she…."

"No, but it's not promising. The doctor confided he doesn't think she'll survive the night. I brought you and the girls here to say your final goodbyes, but I can't tell them that."

Tears streamed out of Brian's eyes like a deflated water balloon. He and Valerie took a seat to decide what the right strategy would be.

"Son, we need to tell them the truth. We have to learn

from the mistakes of the past. We have to lay out all the facts."

"What if she dies, Ma? I can't go through that again."

"If she does, you will have to overcome that tragedy too, except you won't be alone this time. I'll be here for you and the girls."

Brianna and Penny returned from their busy work. Penny skipped down the floor with the folded, plaid blanket bouncing in her arms.

"Give me that before you drop it." Brianna grabbed the blanket from Penny and handed it to Brian. "Here you go, Dad."

"Thanks."

Brianna noticed a change in her father. Although Brian wiped his eyes dry, tears embedded themselves into his blue shirt. This was a red flag for Brianna. "What's wrong with Millicent?"

Brian's voice trembled as he tried to get the words out, "Girls, Mommy's—"

"No! No! No!" Brianna covered her ears to prevent any bad news from penetrating.

Brian tried continuing, "Her brain is not...." However, his feelings conquered him. With his tears resurfacing, he looked to Valerie for strength and tried again. "She's not breathing on—"

"She's not dead. She can't be dead," Brianna screamed as she ran through the double doors to Millicent's room. Brian dropped the blanket, grabbed Penny's hand and they, along with Valerie, chased after her.

Sammy emerged from underneath the tousled blanket. Disoriented from either his stay in the hot vehicle or the tumbles, he made a wobbly attempt to catch up to the family. The doors didn't swing in his favor. Furious that his foolproof plan didn't work, he searched for another point of entry.

Brian, Penny and Valerie caught up to Brianna in Millicent's room, standing over her like an angel. The figure before them wasn't the same Millicent they left yesterday. They watched as the breathing apparatus slowly inflated then deflated. The warm, caramel tone of her skin washed away and refilled with a cold, pale, beige. She hadn't crossed over, but everyone in the room expected she was at the doorstep.

****

The clouds darkened and swelled as if they would give birth to raindrops at any moment. Calverton Memorial soaked in the last sunrays and stood apart from the horizon like a beacon. The strong wind aided in Millicent's strenuous journey. Her fragile bird body declared it was time to give up, but she believed in her spirit, which assured her it wasn't too late.

Millicent landed on a light pole in the parking lot. It wasn't hard for her to spot Brian's SUV parked at an inconsiderate angle. She moved from the pole to the sidewalk past the main entrance and scanned the building to locate her room. "Three up…four from the right…bingo." The window wasn't open but she busted through one today and had no problem with breaking through another.

Millicent leaped into the air but the powerful wind grounded her flight. She tried again, flapping against the wind trying to make ground, only to end back on it. Out of her peripheral, she saw Sammy. They both were airborne, fighting against the current that kept them suspended in the air, going through the motions yet not gaining an inch. Sammy switched direction and Millicent copied. The wind put up an impassable obstacle at every turn, and they ended where they first launched.

"Give up, Small!"

"Never!"

Millicent and Sammy jumped into the air for a third attempt, neither gained an inch.

"We got you, Millicent," Anna informed, still adorned in the silver locket that shined like a ray of hope.

Anna and Gladys positioned themselves behind Millicent and propelled her forward. Their teamwork made Sammy more determined. He flapped his wings so vigorously that he lost feathers, but gained ground. All four sparrows inched closer and closer to the finish line. Before the group could ascend beyond the midpoint of the second floor, the gloomy day turned black and blurry as if the sky produced a shadow that cast over the four sparrows. The change wasn't due to the forecast; instead, it was a massive murder of crows that rushed over Sammy, Millicent, Anna and Gladys with such fury they ruffled the quartet's feathers. The crows encircled the sparrows in a thick, impenetrable bubble and drifted them away from the hospital. Whether the wind calmed or someone opened Millicent's window, it didn't matter. Nothing was getting past the crows.

****

Brianna, Penny, Brian and Valerie formed a semi circle around Millicent's bed.

"What's that, Dad," Brianna asked.

"It's a breathing machine. She can't breathe on her own now; this machine is designed to help her."

"This machine is keeping her alive," Brianna established.

Brian walked to his oldest daughter and held her in his arms. "That and her strong will."

Brianna shrugged her father away. She dragged an

empty chair to Millicent's bedside and sat with her legs bent underneath her. Her upper body slouched over the railing of the bed and her head laid on Millicent's chest. "I never wanted you to die. I love you. Give me a second chance and I'll be obedient. I promised Penny everything would be better. I can't break that promise. I don't want her to hate me for acting like an adult. Why won't you bring her back to us?" Brianna stood up in the chair with her hands fashioned into fists. She demanded answers from the fluorescent lights in the ceiling before dropping back down and planting her face into Millicent's chest. Her sobbing smeared her makeup and transferred it onto the white cast. "Please God, just make it so she finds her way back to us, please."

Brianna's crying was contagious. Like links in a weakened chain, Brian and Valerie wrapped an arm around her and bowed their heads. Hope was no longer present, until Penny made a suggestion.

"If Mommy can't breathe, we need to open a window. That's what she does when my nose is stuffed up." Penny walked to the window, unseen by the rest of the family, and cranked it open.

****

Sammy was the first to attempt to burst through the flock of crows. He scrambled for an exit but his captors crosshatch patterned flying didn't provide an out. Sammy resorted to a familiar tactic. His beak was the key.

"Let me go you crazy birds," Sammy said as he ripped away feathers and flesh. The crows retaliated with double the pain.

"They're going to kill him," Gladys gasped.

"He's already dead," Anna mentioned.

"They're going to kill him again," Gladys added.

"Good," Anna ended.

"Why are they doing this," Millicent asked. "Do they want my life too?"

"I don't think they want to be you Millicent," Gladys responded, "I think they're here for you. Look, they've cleared a way." Gladys showed a void in the wall of crows.

"No, the window's not even open. It has to be a trap," Millicent theorized. "Look at what they're doing to Sammy and he's their friend."

The sparrow's attention turned to Sammy as he continued to fight for his release. His will was strong, but he was severely outnumbered. The crows pecked and clawed at him like fresh road kill until he dropped onto the field beside the hospital. A handful of crows descended with him to ensure he stayed grounded. Down but driven, Sammy strategized another way to fulfill his plan amidst new obstacles.

Millicent wanted to believe Gladys just as much as she wanted to be back in her human form and with her family, but she couldn't handle falling for another trap. "Anna, we can't trust the crows, right?" Millicent waited for Anna to cosign on one of the first orders Anna gave her.

Anna wasn't listening to Millicent. Instead, old thoughts crowded her consciousness. The cleared space was another sign, another confirmation, another opportunity at life meant only for her. Anna waived second-guessing and adhering to rational speech away. She had to seize her moment.

"Sorry, Millicent. I love you Gladys, goodbye," Anna spoke then jetted for the clearing, determined to plow through another window.

"Anna, no," Gladys yelled.

"No," Millicent screamed as she flew after Anna.

Anna was seconds from victory when the crows swooped down on her with the same aggression they dealt

Sammy. She fended them off as best she could and the chain provided some protection but the crows had numbers on their side. Millicent and Gladys quickly spiraled their way underneath dozens of sharp claws to retrieve Anna. From rescue to race for their lives, the sparrows led the crows in an intense chase across the sky.

Sammy observed the chase from his spot on the grass as he rested and contemplated his next plan of attack. The crows that acted as his chaperons left to help the others. Sammy's attention transitioned from the air show to Millicent's room. Her window was open. He couldn't have planned a more perfect diversion.

Sammy catapulted himself into the air headed for his rebirth. The crows sensed his intentions and rallied to stop him. Millicent, Anna and Gladys realized what was happening and joined the melee. It was a free-for-all race with no clear winner in sight.

****

A gust filled the hospital room, rustled the bouquets of flowers, swayed the balloons, whisked Penny's drawing from the wall and sent it floating down like a feather onto Millicent's bed near her feet. Behind the wind, a bird entered the room then vanished as fast as it appeared. Three more birds followed the first.

"Look Daddy, my birds are here!" Penny's voice reverberated with excitement and laughter as she announced the arrival of her gossip partners. Brian, Valerie and Brianna's spirits were too low to look up and notice the visitors. "Hey, where did they go?" Penny went spinning in circles trying to figure out what happened to her feathered friends.

Millicent's eyes fluttered before fully opening. The sight of three, glowing, ghost-like figures standing in front of her bed caught her immediate attention. She identified Anna right away. Beside Anna was a full-figured, older woman—Gladys. Sammy, a short, slender man, stood a few feet to the right of Gladys.

Sandwiched between Brian and Valerie, Brianna clung to her stepmother and recited her true feelings. "I don't want you to die. I love you, Mommy." Before Millicent could respond, Anna answered, "I love you too Brianna, always."

With those last words, another gust of wind blew in and dispersed Anna and Gladys' images into particles of light. Sammy, on the other hand, transformed into a crow and flew out the same way he entered.

"Did you hear that? Dad, Nana, Mom said she loves me." Brianna's eyes along with the eyes of everyone else in the room zeroed in on Millicent's opened eyes.

"Babe, you're awake," Brian stammered. The hopelessness that marked his face replaced with shock and joy.

Penny ran over to her mother's bed. "Mommy, did you see my birds? They followed me here to make sure you were doing better. Did you see them? I drew a picture of them for you up there." Penny pointed to the wall were her artwork once hung. "Where did my picture go?"

"There it is." Valerie pointed to the drawing on the bed decorated with the shiny, silver locket that aided in Millicent's freedom coiled around the neck of one of the birds in Penny's drawing.

"Hey Dad, what's this?" Brianna dangled the necklace in front of everyone's view.

It's your mother's locket from the story I shared with you. I found it in the attic but how did it get here?"

Brianna, remembering what her father told her, couldn't wait to open the locket. She pulled out a piece of yellowed, singed paper, unfolded it with care like a curator handling ancient text, cupped it in the palms of her hands and attempted to read the note aloud. She could only identify the letters E-L-O and what appeared to resemble a V.

Brianna made the connection and solved the mystery, "Love."

Like in kindergarten, Brianna held her mother's love in her hands. She no longer wished for a final goodbye, she was convinced her mother never left.

FUTURE

The sun was up as was Penny. She trotted down the stairs in her favorite flannel pants. It was the middle of July and hot wasn't a strong enough word to describe the outside temperature. Penny balanced her outfit with a tour tank top from one of her favorite bands. She swung open the refrigerator door, took out a container of green juice and poured herself a glass. She returned the container, shut the fridge, opened a bottom cabinet and pulled out a package of birdseeds. She shook a small amount of seeds into a bowl and took it and the juice back upstairs.

In her room, Penny placed the juice and seeds on top of her desk and opened the window. She sprinkled some seeds on the sill then sat in her chair.

"OK Nana, let's see who's worries we can put at ease this week."

"Tweet, tweet…tweet, tweet, tweet."

While she waited, she scrolled through her phone. It wasn't long before another bird landed and began to eat.

"Amanda Abrahe…Charles Donahue…Thomas Sig." Penny gave a short pause between each name to look for a reaction from the bird. She stopped scrolling through the obituaries when her phone rang. "Ugh," Penny sighed as she rejected the call from Brianna. She returned to her task. "Michelle Giek…Omar Stephens…." The bird stood still. "Birdie, are you sure you passed recently?" The bird's head bobbed up and down. "OK, well let me just keep—" Brianna stole Penny's concentration once again. This time it was via text. "You sure have a lot to say this morning don't you, Dear Sister."

Penny ignored Brianna for a second time and carried on with her morning the same as so many mornings before—helping others unable to help themselves.

CALL TO ACTION

I need your help to spread the word about *Penny's Perch*.

1. If you have a website or blog, share how the book touched you. Don't give away the plot, but recommend that they read it and then link to **avoiceinwriting.com**.
2. Write a review for your local paper, favorite magazine, website and Amazon.com.
3. Ask your favorite radio show/news outlet to have **Trina D. Robinson** as a guest. Media people often consider the requests of their listeners/viewers.
4. Talk about the book on email lists, forums and social networking sites. Don't make it an advertisement, but rather share how this book affected your life and offer a link to the site.
5. Stay Connected! Sign-up at **avoiceinwriting.com** to receive the newsletter, blog posts and get information on new releases, events, etc. Also, please follow **Trina D. Robinson** and **A Voice In Writing, LLC** on Facebook.

www.avoiceinwriting.com
FB: @avoiceinwriting
FB: @TrinaDRobinsonTheAuthor

Made in the USA
Columbia, SC
18 April 2022

59058612R00115